The
WICKETT
SISTERS
In Limbo

The
WICKETT
SISTERS
In Limbo

STEPHEN HOUSER

A Novel by Stephen Houser

This is a work of fiction. Names, characters, places,
and incidents either are the product of the author's
imagination or are used fictitiously.

Any resemblance to actual persons, living or dead,
events, or locales is entirely coincidental.

First Printing

Hardcover ISBN: 978-0-9972984-7-5
Softcover ISBN: 978-0-9972984-8-2

Cover Art and Design by Vincent Chong

Printed in the United States of America

In loving memory of teacher
Verna Mae Walter,
who first noted and nourished a spark.

CHAPTER ONE

K ey-rist! Another goddamn strike!" The hugely obese man jumped up and down clapping his fat hands. Grinning at his team, he pointed down the bowling alley at the fallen pins.

"Edward Albert!" a sharp, female voice addressed him from the gallery. The bowler's giddy expression evaporated as he turned around to face the speaker. A short, almost perfectly round old woman dressed in a black dress, a black pillbox hat, and a black veil pulled back over her hair. The stern-looking woman locked eyes with the middle-aged man staring at her.

"Language," she said.

Edward stared at his mother, the iron-willed monarch of nineteenth-century Britain, Alexandrina Victoria. He called her Mum. Everyone else called her Imperial Majesty, or Queen Empress. A few obscure German royals related through her late husband Prince Albert still insisted on appending Princess of Hanover, Duchess of Brunswick and Lunenburg, Princess of Saxe-Coburg and Gotha, and Duchess in Saxony, as if those titles impressed anyone but the leder-hosed animal herders of rural Teutonia ankle deep in goat duty.

Victoria frowned at her son.

"Language," she repeated, in the same stern, disappointed tone she had reserved exclusively for him since his childhood. He deserved it then, and he deserved it now. Edward had always been a royal handful, both as a naughty boy and as a profligate adult. Thank heavens she had not been around to witness the years he'd occupied the throne as Edward VII. But she had heard too many tawdry tales of card playing, smoking, drinking, and adultery to have an unjaundiced view of his years as monarch.

The queen watched her son and nodded toward the little blonde girl in the blue dress sitting next to her. It was Little Mardie Wickett. Her mother Mili was sitting on her other side and watched Edward acknowledge Victoria's point with a slight bow of his head, and then another to Little Mardie in apology for his adult language. For her part, Little Mardie grinned, delighted at the queen's smack-down of her big ass, uncouth, foul-mouthed behemoth of a son.

The prince saw Little Mardie's sarcastic grin and flushed with anger. He wisely turned away, though this effort to hold his tongue came at a cost. His pulse elevated and his blood pressure soared. In life he'd have told both his mother and that little wench to go to Hell. But what was the point of saying that here and now?

Edward turned his attention back to his game. He retrieved his ball from the return and sat down. He had bowled nine strikes in a row. If he finished his tenth frame with a strike, he would be allotted bonus eleventh and twelfth frames. Throwing strikes through those would hand him the Holy Grail of bowling, The Perfect Game.

So exceedingly rare was that elusive crown that the odds of a bowler completing a flawless 300-point game were 11,500 to 1. That number, however, had been calculated on Earth, where such hallowed games had been witnessed and recorded. The odds against it in Hell were infinitely higher, perhaps even incalculable, for The Perfect Game had never happened down here.

In fact, a perfect score in *any* sport in Hell had never happened. Not ever. Not for anyone. Golfers did not recover from bogeys. Tennis volleys never rose above love forty. Competitive swimmers never saw the number ten. And bowlers, even the best ones, never bowled The Perfect Game.

Nonetheless, Edward couldn't help but imagining himself throwing all strikes for the tenth, eleventh, and twelfth frames. He chatted excitedly with his teammates, everyone voicing their encouragement. None of them had ever achieved anything close to Edward's brilliant score in this quarterfinal series against The American Presidents, but as a team they had played so well that Edward only had to roll a spare in the tenth frame to make the Royals victorious.

The American Presidents sat on the other side of the ball return watching the Brits prepare for their final round. Though the Americans were facing elimination from further championship play, they were also enchanted with Edward's unique opportunity to bowl Hell's first Perfect Game. Woodrow Wilson was drinking tea and waiting, his long legs crossed like two matchsticks in slacks. Thomas Jefferson, dressed in a long blue coat with a gorgeous white silk shirt, was smiling and smoking hemp. Franklin Roosevelt looked casually elegant, leaning back in his wheelchair and drinking a ginger ale, and John Kennedy had turned all the way around in his seat so he could give Mili the once over.

Mili ignored him and watched Edward puff on his cigar. What a fat oaf, she thought. Yet she had heard way more than enough rumors to believe that his reputation as a womanizer was true. Fat or not, he was apparently able to woo adoring females into his bed with witty conversation and rapt attention. God knew that worked. *She* knew that worked.

Lucifer was the most charming conversationalist she had ever met. He was innocent, suggestive, aloof, provocative, brilliant, self-effacing, and flattering all in one package. Plus, he was gorgeous. She glanced at him, seated between the two competition lanes as contest judge, and found herself as enchanted as ever by his angelic face and those blonde curls cascading over his shoulders. She wondered if instead of appearing as a serpent in the Garden of Eden he had actually shown up as his handsome self. One had to believe *that* was who Eve had fallen for. It would explain a lot of stuff that got blamed on the apple.

Mili turned her attention back to the bowlers. The British Royals were queuing up for their last round starting with Henry VIII. He was seated in an elaborate wooden wheelchair that two of his teammates rolled up to the alley foul line. The Tudor king was tailored sumptuously in a gold-threaded silk and crimson cotton coat with matching pantaloons. His legs were left bare to prevent the pant legs from rubbing against his ulcerated skin, a no man's land of oozing carbuncles and scabbing sores.

He had suffered from such lesions most of his adult life and had brought an abundant collection of them to Hell after his overworked heart failed at age fifty-five. The same number, incidentally, as the measure of his waistline. What an oddly wonderful coincidence Mili thought, pondering whether or not the rabid Kabbalah fans down here had managed to make anything of that.

Henry's weight made it impossible for him to stand or walk, but he could still bowl. He was handed his bowling ball, which he proceeded to toss with a vigor that belied his fat-boy appearance. He struck down all the pins for a final score of 267. He nodded at Edward modestly, knowing that the real hero of the day would be his distant successor.

Mili gazed at Little Mardie sitting in the chair next to her. She was avidly following the match, although in-between frames she was on her iPad, her thirteenth birthday present. She was growing tall, already over five foot five in height. She was a very slim girl, revealing no hints yet of what her hips or breasts would look like when developed.

What was clear already, however, was that she would be a beautiful young woman with a perfect oval face, a small nose, bright blue eyes, and gorgeous blonde hair. She was wearing her favorite dress, her Alice Blue Gown, as she called it. She wore it on every occasion she wanted to feel like a princess, which at her age was just about every day.

She reminded Mili very much of how her own mother had looked when she was very young, though that was not something she had ever spoken about with her twin Mardie. She had forgiven her sister for their childhood conflicts involving both parents, and now the sisters observed an unbroken nothing-spoken-out-loud pact concerning their respective relationships with mum and da. Hopefully that vow would continue to safeguard their reconciliation.

Mili watched her daughter cheer the bowlers with demonic glee. Little Mardie resembled her father in so many ways, yet to Mili's knowledge she had never asked him about his ancient life in Heaven as the Archangel of Light. Or his so-called *fall* from God's grace. Nor, for that matter, had Little Mardie expressed any interest in Mili's past. She wasn't sure her daughter knew even one speck about her career as a homicide detective at London's Scotland Yard.

Little Mardie did not seem to be particularly interested in other people's lives, though an exception was her fascination with Alice Roosevelt Longworth, the acid-tongued daughter of Theodore Roosevelt. Alice had bloomed into a very pretty young woman during her father's presidency, and her beauty and impetuous behavior fascinated the American public.

In her day, she shot revolvers from trains, smoked cigarettes in public, and even jumped into a swimming pool fully clothed, which prompted John Kennedy's brother Bobby to teasingly chide her years later for her outrageous behavior. She responded haughtily that his rebuke was nonsensical. Her conduct would only have been outrageous if she'd taken her clothes off first.

Little Mardie absolutely adored the old woman, now a Grand Dame in Hell, and had fallen in love with her signature blue dresses, the originals on which her own Alice Blue Gown was based. Alice was equally enchanted by Little Mardie, and whenever she came by to visit, Alice patted the pillow on the chair next to hers embroidered with the words, **If you don't have anything nice to say about anyone, come**

sit by me. Little Mardie was as headstrong as Alice had ever been. And, for that matter, she was just as headstrong as her father, Lucifer.

While Lucifer had made some strides in controlling his somewhat ferocious temper, his daughter let hers loose frequently, albeit not *quite* as frequently lately, after burning down the new bedroom addition at her Aunt Mardie's house where she had thrown a pyrotechnic fit over chocolate-dipped cake balls she had been denied.

Her original Alice Blue Gown had burned completely off leaving her standing nude on the lawn watching the corner of her aunt's house burn down. Such humiliation she intended never to experience again. The nude part anyway. Lucifer and Mili granted her wish for a new Alice Blue Gown, hoping it would remind her to control her temper.

Her father had confessed to her that controlling his own temper had enabled him to wear regular clothes, allowing him to eschew the fireproof robes he'd previously worn. He did not mention, however, that his office was still decorated with asbestos furnishings, work being the only place where he still allowed himself a flame-up, as he termed it, when an occasion called for it.

Mili turned her attention back to the bowling match. The British Royals were running through their rotation leading up to Albert's tenth frame. The current bowler was the Royals' second-seeded player and first-seeded gossip, Henry VIII's daughter, Elizabeth I. Or Liz as everyone called her behind her back. The Virgin Queen was skinny as a stick, bald and red-faced, with out-of-control rosacea bumps and rashes. And she truly *was* a virgin, having discovered at a young age that what she enjoyed most about a man was what he carried between his ears, not what he displayed between his legs.

To protect herself from the inevitable predatory royal males who sought her hand hoping to rule her country, she'd invented the myth that she was married to England. Therefore she had no need for a mortal spouse (to fuck *or* fuck things up). Her ingenious stunt had worked, resounding magnificently through the centuries since her death, on Earth *and* in Hell.

It was an impressive spin for a woman living in the sixteenth century. Liz had darting green eyes and a quick laugh, and she and Mili shared tea together frequently. The woman knew everything about anybody who was a somebody, and gossiped with verve and delight. All in all, she was as pleasant an informer as Mili had ever encountered.

Despite her billowing skirt covering who knew how many petticoats, Elizabeth danced down to the lane's foul line and released her ball with power and panache. It glided straight down the center of the lane and hit the front pin with an audible blow. Alas, one of the pins in a far corner refused to bow down to the queen, but she nabbed the knave with a quick spare.

Her proud father gave her a thumbs-up, and Edward flashed her an A-Okay with his thumb and forefinger. Liz laughed out loud, knowing that Edward's gesture actually meant asshole, and that he was suggesting a sport he wanted to play with her besides bowling.

Mili turned her attention back to Victoria's son. Edward was smoking a long, fat, cigar, no doubt a suggestive symbol of his baser impulses. Though his turn was the one everybody was waiting for, a last frame still preceded Edward's belonging to Charles II. Oddly, the king was not anywhere on the floor.

From the team bench Liz caught Mili's eye and nodded toward the men's room behind the bar. Mili grinned, realizing by the way Liz tossed her head, that the randy monarch was *not* in there by himself. Good Lord. What kind of testosterone did these Brits possess?

Her eyes wandered over to Lucifer again, seated elegantly on a high stool wearing a black-and-white striped judge's shirt and black slacks. He was sitting between the two lanes the bowlers were using. On either side of him stood a Samn demon. Lucifer called them referees and made them wear black-and-white striped shirts, too, but with gray slacks. In actuality, they were bouncers. As the official whose word was absolute and final, Satan had perched himself with his legs crossed, patiently abiding the snail's pace exhibited by the Royals. He felt Mili looking at him.

He turned and glanced at her. She yanked her head in the direction of the men's loo and rolled her eyes. He smiled, but gave her no more reaction than that, mainly because he could care less what King Charles II was up to in the men's room. Lucifer was happy just being here at the championship series he organized every year, as thrilled as a youngster to be observing the climax of the bowling league season.

Lucifer loved bowling. And he loved this venue. It was a cheerful emporium that he had carefully patterned on American bowling alleys built in the 1950s. They were welcoming men's retreats where World War II vets could bowl and down a few Pabst Blue Ribbon beers, having left their wives and baby boomer offspring at home eating TV dinners and watching *I Love Lucy*.

This bowling alley, Avalon Lanes, was done in pastel pinks and blues and boasted two dozen pristine lanes with a viewers' gallery. There was a mahogany bar with stools and a dozen pink Formica tables and chairs. The lanes were maple, and the rest of the bowling alley floors were laid in colorful polka-dot linoleum. It reminded Mili of a Wonder Bread wrapper.

Satan had constructed a half-dozen bowling alleys identical to Avalon. Although scarcely a thing ever went wrong with any of them, he had crews of demons on twenty-four-hour alert ready to service, repair, or replace anything in any alley, *instantly*. It was an extraordinary commitment to harmonious enterprise, especially considering the contrary nature of Hell. But all of Lucifer's bowling alleys were flawlessly run and maintained.

The same was true of the small house Lucifer shared with his wife and their daughter. He loved their family's abode now that bodies were no longer being dumped on its porch. It was a cozy, comfortably furnished home where the three of them lived very happily together.

It was also the only home in Hell—besides the one belonging to Mili's twin Mardie—where air conditioning had been installed. It proved that nepotism was almost as old as God, and certainly as old as his one-time Archangel of Light, Lucifer Morningstar.

Mili entertained a lot of folks in her home, though not as many as her sister. Mardie hosted three separate reading clubs, regularly threw dinner parties for actors performing in the Good News Club's biblical reenactments, and over the years had cultivated an extensive social network of wonderful characters from across human history who were always dropping in for coffee or tea.

For a woman in her sixties, she also displayed a fabulous libido, which until settling down with Bowles from the Good News Club, had driven her to wade into a stream of boyfriends, happily shrieking her way through their sexual congress. Mardie herself had never told Mili about any of that. But Liz had.

Satan's own social network included visitors from Heaven. Angels and Archangels who remembered Lucifer. They frequently detoured to stop down and see him. Gabriel, Michael, and Raphael had all been to tea at his home. They never failed to be amused when he politely, but persistently, challenged them to join a bowling competition, even offering his own outstanding bowling skills as a fourth member of their team. They grinned and always declined.

Possibly, Mili thought secretly, that despite their outward collegiality, the Archangels had scruples about accepting their disgraced colleague as a teammate. Satan's own take was that the angels didn't want to get their cloud-soft asses kicked by the bad boys and girls bowling on the top teams down here. Mili leaned toward her husband's ass-kicking view. All in all, it wasn't an unreasonable reason to decline bowling in Hell.

Charles finally exited the restroom and sauntered over to his bowling lane. He was wearing gold pants and a crimson Royals shirt, with gold and crimson shoes to match. The handsome monarch went to the ball return rack and picked up his ball. Mili knew that despite his laid-back persona he was a serious man. He'd grown up during a time of civil war in England, and his father King Charles I had been overthrown and beheaded by Parliament's leader, Oliver Cromwell.

Restored to the throne by a repentant population, his son Charles II had been a sober and devoted king, absolutely separating his royal responsibilities from his frequent philandering toward which everyone turned a blind eye, except his wife. Story was that when she'd heard he'd picked flowers from a public park for one of his mistresses, she ordered all the flowers to be ripped out and never replanted. So it was, and so it remained, called Green Park to this day.

Mili wondered why Charles' queen wasn't actually relieved that her randy mate found other outlets for his excess testosterone other than her royal person. You'd think she'd be glad it wasn't *her* skirt being thrown up ten times a day.

Charles lifted his bowling ball to his chest, walked straight to the alley, and tossed it vigorously. It flew like the wind and made a resounding strike. Charles bowed his head to acknowledge the raucous cheers from Liz, Henry, and Edward, as well as the hundreds of Royals fans in the gallery.

At last all eyes turned to Edward. The tenth and final frame of the tournament had arrived and it was his. Could he roll a strike and be given eleventh and twelfth frames to attempt to bowl Hell's first Perfect Game? Edwards stood up. It was showtime.

CHAPTER TWO

Satan stood up and raised his hand.

"Ladies and Gentlemen," he said to the teams and their fans. "I am calling a five-minute recess to allow his majesty Edward time to prepare his mind and body for the greatest frame of his bowling career." There was a distinct groan of despair in the bowling alley. "Tut, tut," Lucifer chided mildly. "We can all wait a few minutes while Edward prepares to attempt Hell's first Perfect Game. Get a drink. Use the restroom. The climax of this semifinal match will happen soon enough." There was murmuring, and to many in the room it seemed as though Satan was attempting to jinx Edward by requiring this dramatic delay before his last frame.

Mili scanned the Presidents' team hoping that John Kennedy had found someone else to stare at. He had. Little Mardie was now in his sights. Mili frowned. Thanks to Liz, the queen-in-the-know, she was all too aware that JFK's extracurricular sexual activities in Hell made Victoria's son Edward look inept.

John got laid everywhere and anywhere, indoors and out, only forgoing places where he might get thorns in his backside, the latter being a concern because Jack always insisted on being on the bottom according to those who'd been on the top. He claimed it was because of his damaged back. More likely it was due to his lazy dick. Mili shook her head. Jack looked at her and winked. Thank heavens her daughter was still too young for him to approach. There were some boundaries, even in Hell.

"Tea, my darlings?" It was Queen Victoria. She smiled sweetly at Little Mardie, and nodded at Mili.

"Does it come with cookies?" Little Mardie asked.

Victoria chuckled, and her eyes sparkled.

"For you, dear, it comes with oatmeal cookies slathered wickedly thick with vanilla frosting." The queen eyed Mili, then added, "If your mum allows, that is."

Mili nodded, always appreciative of the queen's thoughtfulness toward her daughter. They visited together every time Edward played at Avalon Lanes. She felt sorry that Victoria had not been reunited at her death with her late husband, Prince Albert. The good Lutheran Prince had gone to Heaven and was probably hobnobbing at this very moment with the likes of Martin Luther and Philip Melanchthon, though the brilliant engineer would be equally comfortable chatting with Sir Christopher Wren or Frank Lloyd Wright, architects like himself, who had left remarkably original buildings behind in their earthly wake.

Victoria beckoned to a server at the bar, a man who looked an awful lot like Russia's Gregori Yefimovich Rasputin. He came over immediately, a bone-thin, depressed-looking man with a scraggly beard and hanging bags beneath his eyes. He was dressed in wrinkled black work pants and a stained white cafeteria-style smock. He took the queen's order for tea and oatmeal cookies (with extra frosting) and bustled off.

Lucifer waved at Little Mardie. She waved back, then ran down to see him. She wrapped her arms around his waist and hugged him with all of her might. Satan smiled with delight. He bent down and kissed her on the forehead, right where her beautiful blonde hair met the flawless, pale skin of her face.

"How are you, cupcake?" he asked, looking into her eyes.

"Bored to death, Daddy," she shot back. "Knocking the pins over is great, but all the stuff in between is awful. Nothing happens. How can you stand it?"

"Ah," Lucifer answered. "You need to learn to savor the suspense, the anticipation—"

"—the boredom," Little Mardie interrupted. "Daddy, it's killing me."

"Someday you will find it *absorbing*," he told her, then observed the not-a-chance-in-Hell expression on her petulant face. "Just maybe not today," he conceded.

Little Mardie didn't respond, but did give her father a peck on the cheek when he leaned over seeking that very thing.

"Thank you, angel," he said.

Little Mardie smiled and gave him another kiss. Lucifer returned to his stool. She ran back to the gallery to drink her tea and dig into the tray of frosted cookies.

Edward tamped the ash from his cigar into an ashtray sitting on top of the ball return rack, then clenched it in his teeth. He looked down the alley. Sixty feet away stood the ten pins that held his destiny. His face was intense, his bearing rigid. A single strike was all that separated him from bowling glory. Edward glanced respectfully at the judge. Lucifer nodded gravely.

Edward bent over and picked up his bowling ball, then positioned himself a few paces behind the foul line. He held the ball against his chest. No matter what happened next, for one glorious moment he possessed the undivided attention of everyone in the gallery. He savored it all right down to the tip of his cigar.

Then Edward made a move that astounded the Royals, the Presidents, the visitors, and the Lord of Hell himself. He shifted the ball to his left hand—a hand he never bowled with—put his fingers into the drilled holes, and gripped it firmly. He stepped toward the lane, and with a graceful swing of his left arm he released the ball. It rolled down the alley, hooking ever so slightly to the left, then curved right just shy of true center and hit the head pin. Every single pin flew off the floor.

Edward stood still and stared. Everyone had jumped to their feet when the ball swerved toward the head pin and now stood frozen in disbelief. Edward spun toward the judge's chair and looked at Lucifer. The Devil was also on his feet trying to comprehend what had just happened. He looked at Edward, then back at the toppled pins in the lane. Edward had thrown a strike. His tenth strike.

He had earned the two bonus frames. The crowd came alive, cheering, whistling, and crying out Edward's name. The record-breaking bowler nodded to the crowd, then seemingly without even taking a breath hurled two additional strikes leaving the last ten pins spinning at the end of the lane.

Lucifer couldn't speak. What had just happened? His mind raced searching for possible answers. Had Edward's brief break somehow neutralized the physics Jehovah had set in place here in Hell? Or had Edward's flippant, even disdainful, switch of hands break up or break off Heaven's eternal prohibitions against scoring ten—let alone twelve—strikes in a row?

The crowd went wild. Lucifer shook his head in amazement. Son of a gun. Edward, Prince of Wales, King of England, and resident of Hell had bowled The Perfect Game. Satan raised his hand to quiet the ecstatic crowd. They settled down, waiting for him to speak.

"Bowlers, ladies and gentlemen," he began. "Edward has rolled twelve balls in a row and achieved a strike with each one, winning the semifinal match for The British Royals. Of greater significance, I dare say, is that he has bowled the very first Perfect Game in the history of this sport in Hell." The crowd went crazy, screaming Edward's name. Lucifer looked at him and bowed slightly from the waist.

The Royals team surged forward, clapping Edward on the back. Elizabeth I went so far as to hug him, and Henry VIII held Edward's arm high up in the air. Satan waded through the happy throng, shook Edward's hand, and offered his congratulations. Everyone cheered the historic victor, ecstatic about the prince's triumph. No one questioned *why* it had finally occurred. Except Lucifer, and *he* was struck with terrible anxiety.

This Perfect Game should never have happened. Something had broken down here for it occur, and he had no idea what it was. He looked at the gallery and found Mili. Her eyes were hooded, disguising her fears, but Lucifer instinctively knew that she, too, was aware that something in Hell had gone terribly wrong.

But then hope burst into his troubled heart. His magnificent wife could unravel this mystery if anyone could, uncovering what had happened and helping him understand what was going on. He lifted his hand and waved at her. She saw him and their eyes locked. How he loved her. How he needed her.

Then Lucifer frowned. Where was Little Mardie? Mili was standing by Queen Victoria, but his daughter had vanished. He scanned the gallery for the girl in the Alice Blue Gown, always easy to find, yet suddenly she was nowhere to be seen. He walked toward Mili, his eyes searching for Little Mardie as he did.

"Hello," Little Mardie cheerfully announced, appearing in front of her father just as he reached Mili and Queen Victoria. Lucifer took his daughter by the shoulders. Little Mardie knit her brows, bracing herself for the worst.

"Where were you?" the Devil asked sternly. "I was so worried."

"There's a hole at the end of the bar," she said. "I stepped into it—"

"Don't say by accident," her father warned.

"—and I looked around," Mardie finished. She went dead silent seeing the first telltale flames of her father's explosive temper pop up on top of his head.

Mili stepped in, calm and supportive.

"And what did you see?" she asked.

"It's too loud to talk here," Little Mardie complained.

"I agree," Mili replied. "Let's go find a quiet place."

Mili, dressed in red shorts and a cream-colored cotton blouse, took Little Mardie's hand and walked off. Lucifer watched them leave, still upset, but not so upset that he couldn't appreciate his wife's small waist and perfect behind. He thought Mili's Hellion body was smoking hot, and while she teased him sometimes for designing it that way, she never complained that he had. God had invented sex. But Lucifer had invented sexy.

Mili led Little Mardie to the gallery bar on the opposite side of the bowling alley, far from Prince Albert and his adoring fans, yet very near where her daughter said she had stepped into a black hole. Little Mardie and Mili sat down. Lucifer, following a bit behind them, went to the bar to fetch a cold Coca Cola for Little Mardie and a bottle of sparkling mineral water for his wife. Mili resumed questioning her daughter.

"So what did you see, sweetheart?" she asked, making sure she sounded like a mom, and not like a Scotland Yard detective.

"I stepped out onto a hill," she began. "A very big hill that overlooked a city with tall silver buildings far below. There was the ocean, and bays, and bridges to cross them."

Mili thought of New York, Sydney, and Lisbon, but her daughter could have been anywhere in any universe. Holes in space went everywhere.

"What else, angel?"

"There was a tall tower next to me made of metal. It was very ugly, I thought. Also, one of the bridges was painted orange and its towers poked up through the fog sitting on top of it."

"I think you were by the city of San Francisco," Mili told her. "You were on one of the tall peaks that rise up behind the city, looking down on everything. Can you show me where the hole is that took you there?"

"It's right there," she said, pointing toward the end of the bar. Loud, happy laughter echoed through the bowling alley, and when Edward and his increasingly boisterous fans spotted Lucifer, they began to chant, "Satan! Satan! Satan!" The Devil looked over. Kings, queens, and presidents lifted champagne glasses, beckoning him to come back and join them.

"Go," Mili told him. "You know the gist of what happened, and the fact is, Little Mardie is safe and sound right here with us."

Lucifer gave them their drinks and left. Truth was, he was glad to get away. He was having terrible difficulties focusing on Little Mardie's wormhole adventure. Edward's feat was all that he could think about. Troubling, difficult questions filled his mind. Eternal laws had governed life down here for countless millennia and ensured that *nothing* was perfect. Yet Edward had bowled The Perfect Game. In front of a mass of witnesses, no less. How could this have happened? What had changed? Change was not his friend. Not down here.

Lucifer forced himself to smile as he approached the revelers. He reached out to accept a glass of champagne from Franklin Roosevelt, another monarch who bowled from a wheelchair. The president eyed Lucifer warily, despite his happy-days-are-here-again smile. The Devil admired Roosevelt's perfectly pressed slacks, his crisp white shirt, and his light blue sweater vest. FDR was always turned out well, but what Satan admired far more than FDR's sartorial excellence, was his brilliant Machiavellian mind, absolutely free of any qualms about working behind the scenes or fighting in back alleys to get things done. He would have made a great ruler of Hell. Lucifer toasted Roosevelt and enjoyed one brief moment unperturbed by worries about Edward's Perfect Game.

It didn't last.

CHAPTER THREE

I t's right there," Little Mardie said, pointing the toe of her patent leather shoe straight ahead.

"Are you sure?" Mili asked, seeing only Wonder Bread linoleum.

"I'm sure," Little Mardie insisted. "I can see *into* it from right here."

"What do you see?"

"A shadowy opening like the mouth of a cave."

Mili was not pleased at what she heard.

"And you just walked into that?" she asked a bit tartly. "Having no any idea where it went, or whether you'd ever be able to return?" Mili didn't add the other remark churning in head. We were lost over the rainbow once before, don't you remember?

Little Mardie gazed at her mother, remaining calm in the face of Mili's maternal worry.

"The fact is, Mom, I went to a beautiful place on Earth and came back." She looked at her mother, wearing a reasonable expression to match her tone. "And you can, too." Without waiting for a response, Little Mardie stood up and pulled her mother's hand. Both she and Mili stepped into the hole and stepped out onto a tall hill overlooking San Francisco. A mountain really. They were at least two thousand feet up and a salty sea breeze whipped the summit. Clouds, fog, and patches of sunshine cast magic shadows on the famous city, set like a diamond in the crest of the peninsula below.

Little Mardie threw her arms up in the air and cried, "Woo-hoo!" She looked at her mother, who grinned with exuberance. Little Mardie took her mother's hands again and they danced in circles, laughing and shouting. Mili laughed with abandon, astonished at the feelings she was experiencing. And then she knew why. It was the feeling of being alive, truly alive, perched above a place where there were oceans to be seen, mountains to be climbed, and a beautiful city to be explored. It was the feeling of freedom. The feeling that life was full of choices, opportunities, and adventures.

There was nothing like this in Hell because every choice and every experience was shrunken and poisoned. There was no freedom in Hell. There was just *hell* in Hell. Mili determined that this unexpected moment of happiness would not be squandered no matter what the consequences would be.

"How would you like to go down and see San Francisco?" Mili asked Little Mardie.

Her daughter burst out laughing again, happy beyond even Mili's feelings of rapture.

"Do you mean it?" Little Mardie cried.

"If you're sure you can help us find our way back," Mili cautioned.

"I can!" Little Mardie exclaimed. "It's the only hole on top of this big hill. If we can get back to this hill, I can find the hole!"

"All right," Mili told her. "I have always wanted to crack crab and drink a glass of wine at Fisherman's Wharf."

"And I want Ben and Jerry's Cherry Garcia ice cream!" Little Mardie shouted.

Mili smiled at her daughter.

"What kind of ice cream, honey?"

"Cherry Garcia. Vanilla ice cream and cherries. Jerry Garcia told me that it was named after him. I wish he could try some."

"Maybe we'll just have to bring him here sometime," Mili responded.

"Holy shit!" Little Mardie said. "Really?"

"Excuse me?" her mother asked, not appreciating that that particular expression had already found its way into her thirteen-year-old daughter's lexicon.

"Sorry," Little Mardie said, and meant it.

"We're not in Hell," was Mili's take.

"People on Earth don't swear?"

"Not like they do in Hell."

"Wow," Little Mardie said, impressed. "Can we go explore now?"

"We can," Mili answered, smiling again.

"May I also buy some Hard Rock Café pins?" Little Mardie asked, her eyes growing big and hopeful. "You know, one of Fishermans' Wharf. And maybe one of the Golden Gate Bridge?"

"Yes, you may, if you can take them back through the space hole," Mili replied. "*And* you make sure that your father doesn't see them right away."

* * *

Lucifer was walking from the bowling alley to his downtown office. He didn't usually walk, because he didn't like to walk. He was forced to watch out for all the crap that jerks tossed onto the sidewalks—broken beer bottles, food wrappers, shredded tires, abandoned bikes—whatever you could trip over was lying on the sidewalks.

If someone really wanted to make things better down here, they could clean up all that stuff. He had a whole slew of hedge fund managers showing up these days and this might be just the task for them. Problem was, it would make them feel better about themselves, and that wasn't what Hell was all about. You could have your fun, certainly, but the game wasn't about penance. It was about punishment.

Lucifer stopped and looked down a crack in the sidewalk. A full-grown dandelion had somehow managed to grow out of a broken patch, sending its roots into the soil below and producing a healthy plant with sturdy yellow petals, and a full, perfect, black heart. The Devil stared at it. He had never witnessed anything like this before. This sort of thing didn't happen. *This sort of thing wasn't supposed to happen.*

The soil in Hell was poor and whatever tried to grow in it was stunted and sickly. People still tried to raise what they could, harvesting tomatoes that looked like gargoyles, cucumbers that were shaped like shriveled-up pipe organ cacti, and berries whose skins were crinkly like raisins. The folks who grew such monstrosities ate them and sold them, even though they tasted pretty much as bad as they looked. Half-assed, Hellish versions of the real thing. Punishment, reiterated ad nauseam.

Lucifer squatted down and gazed at the dandelion. Son of a bitch. It was young and healthy. And not more than a couple of days old. It was the kind of dandelion Ray Bradbury would have worn in his lapel and then pressed in a book. What the Hell? Something was *really* wrong down here. First, The Perfect Game, and now this perfect flower. Maybe the flower would have been first if he had gone out earlier. Didn't matter. Fucked was fucked, and he was not happy.

Hell was his domain and nothing had changed for the better for tens of thousands of years. Oh, sure, there were *new* things once in a while, like the Baptists and their biblical reenactments, but dressing up in costumes and playing at Bible stories didn't bring about any fundamental changes. The Perfect Game was *new*. And the perfect dandelion was new. And these things could and would change Hell. They should never be welcome.

Lucifer reached down and plucked the dandelion. He could give it to his daughter who had never seen a real flower. He imagined her smile when he handed it to her. What a sweet moment that would be. Satan shook his head wistfully. Some things were just not meant to be down here, and that's how it was. He stood up, dropped the dandelion on the sidewalk, and crushed it with the sole of his shoe.

He wiped the sweat from the back of his neck with his handkerchief and looked up at the sky. Slowly, but surely, the gray clouds were separating, and to the Devil's amazement—for the first time he could ever recall—blue sky cracked through the ever-present haze. And there, by God, was the sun in all its glory. Lucifer stared in disbelief. Blue skies? Sun? His world was falling apart.

* * *

Mili and Little Mardie walked along the road that wound down and around the mountain. A city sign named it Mount Sutro. The peak was tall and dignified, with rows of old Victorian cottages clinging to its sides. Each was painted in gaudy colors and boasted lawns and gardens landscaped within an inch of Heaven's standards.

The combination was charming, only gradually giving way to row houses and multi-story commercial structures as they walked into downtown San Francisco. Eve then the city streets were clean, and the old stone buildings wonderfully decorated with rainbow-painted facades and plaster molding.

"This doesn't look much like New Babylon, does it?" Mili asked Little Mardie, who'd been silently taking everything in. Her daughter shook her head no. Bright sunshine. Blue sky. Grassy slopes. A prosperous and well-cared for city. It didn't make Little Mardie think less of Hell because it was not the same as San Francisco. But it did strike her that living in such a lovely place must make the residents very, very happy.

Having roamed through Hell with her father simply emphasized that San Francisco was not your normal city. She'd met a ton of damned souls from Los Angeles who couldn't tell the difference between the City of Angels on Earth and New Babylon in Hell. San Francisco was different. It was special.

23

Mili and Little Mardie headed for the center of town, encountering a lot of colorfully dressed characters along the way. There was a young man with blonde dreadlocks wearing nothing more than a black pirate's hat and a flesh-colored thong. Two middle-aged men in nuns' attire were rollerblading. A few business people, dressed in conventional suits and dresses, were walking urgently to important destinations. There were a lot of twenty-somethings wearing checked or plaid shirts, slacks, and Frank Sinatra hats. And crowds of tourists sporting shorts and T-shirts were everywhere, speaking a myriad of tongues including *English* English, much to Mili's delight.

There were homeless people too, sitting, standing, smoking, and peeing. Mili stopped and talked to each one—except the man peeing—and put an American twenty-dollar bill in every outstretched hand. In turn she received earnest messages of "God bless you." Not bloody likely, Mili thought, but she appreciated the sentiment.

Mili suspected that there were demons out and about in the city as well, camouflaged in various disguises. She didn't like those bastards, but the ones engaged in smuggling were usually hard workers and honest. Go figure. Pfotenhauer, her charming chauffeur, who had been a key stoolie in her Scotland Yard days, was friends with many of the miscreants who crisscrossed folded space between Hell and Earth, smuggling back illegal, but welcome, contraband.

The former mobster claimed that many of these demons morphed themselves into Chinese businessmen whom San Franciscans honored and respected for their ability to deliver the goods. Pfotenhauer also revealed that a lot of the demons engaged in black market traffic were gay and therefore possessed an additional recreational reason to visit San Francisco. She doubted, however, that those particular chaps morphed into Asian merchants.

Mili ate Dungeness crab at Fisherman's Wharf and leaned on a railing where she could watch the boats returning from beyond the Golden Gate Bridge, loaded with rock cod, snapper, sardines, and shark.

"Can we go now?" Little Mardie asked, finishing a box of French fries. "It smells funny here." She wrinkled up her nose.

Mili didn't think it did, but on they went, heading along the waterfront for Pier 39 and the Hard Rock Café. Little Mardie bought a handful of Hard Rock pins and checked out every piece of rock and roll memorabilia displayed on the café walls—from signed guitars to framed gold and platinum albums—while rock music pounded from speakers planted in every corner and cranny of the place.

Food flashed by on big trays hauled around by terrifically strong, smiling girls from the Orient. They wore short skirts and tall heels—beautiful Japanese, Thai, Chinese, Cambodian, and Filipina females—carting platters of tourist food cooked in deep fat fryers.

"Can we go?" Mili asked her daughter after a while. "It smells funny here."

Little Mardie laughed out loud and headed for the door. She strolled up the pier in search of ice cream, carrying two large Hard Rock bags that didn't slow her down for a nanosecond. She spotted a stand that sold Ben and Jerry's. She ordered the biggest waffle cone the vendor had, then sat down on a bench and ate her Cherry Garcia.

Mili ordered a cup of *Late Night Snack*, a vanilla bean ice cream with a salted caramel swirl and fudge-covered potato chip pieces. OMG she thought as she ate. If she had discovered this when she had still been alive her diabetes would have subtracted every one of her digits and continued from there.

"Did you know that Ben Cohen and Jerry Greenfield, the founders of Ben and Jerry's, are social activists?" Little Mardie asked.

"I thought they just made ice cream," Mili answered.

"They have principles for their company," Little Mardie went on.

"Like using natural ingredients?" Mili responded.

"Yes, but more importantly, they make commitments to recycle, to pay their employees a living wage, and to support socially responsible issues like marriage equality. Ben and Jerry are trying to be fair to the Earth, the folks who make their ice cream, and the consumers who eat it. Once upon a time, people on Earth called that *quality of life* awareness."

"Nice," Mili agreed. "But that kind of social conscience can't really apply to where we live, can it?" She was not trying to be discouraging, but she knew full well that none of the worthwhile activities that Little Mardie had described mattered one wit in Hell.

"No," Little Mardie said understanding, "but they should."

Mili gazed at her daughter. Where was this wellspring of social justice coming from? Little Mardie had never ever been required or even encouraged to think about anything or anyone beyond the wellbeing of her own family. They had cars that didn't break down, air conditioning that worked, and food that was brought in special.

Little Mardie had had very little exposure as to how most souls in Hell faced heat and filth without the privilege of clean water and fresh food. It was true that some folks in Hell were well off, making fortunes down there just like they'd made on Earth, forming clandestine business contracts with demons to smuggle in liquor, cigarettes, food, clothes, jewelry, and art.

Men like William Randolph Hearst and Cornelius Vanderbilt experienced no real difference between Hell and the luxurious lives they led at Hearst Castle or The Breakers. However, for each well-off resident of Hell, there were millions of citizens whose lives were nightmares of debilitating heat and desperate shortages. They were living lives where one could starve yet not die, suffer from disease or disability with no hope of relief, and face an eternal day-to-day existence without a single moment of laughter, hope, or happiness.

Mili watched Little Mardie finish her ice cream. Mili ate another spoonful of her own and wondered what, if anything, she could do about comforting the people in Hell. Perhaps she could start with a meaningful personal gesture. Like vowing to forgo any more ice cream until it was available to *everyone* down there. Although, maybe she should just promise herself that she wouldn't have any more *Ben and Jerry's* until such a time. Or maybe she should just not eat ice cream when she was thinking about how she could improve the lot of the damned. Yes. Yes. That was it. She nodded solemnly, and licked her spoon.

CHAPTER FOUR

D oes being naked make me look fat?" Mardie asked her sister. She was sitting in the tub, chest deep in the water, shaving her legs. Mili perched on the toilet seat watching her. Mardie propped her right foot on the tile wall at the head of the tub and cropped off the hairs on her leg with long, smooth strokes. She rubbed her hand along her calf.

It was smooth, temporarily denied the luxurious stubble it had managed to grow in the three days since last Saturday when she had shaved it off anticipating a quality check from Bowles, her darkly handsome bartender. She'd passed his inspection.

She rubbed her calf a second time. She wanted to pass again tonight. Which would be particularly nice since Josephine Baker was playing the Queen of Sheba in the reenactment *Solomon and Sheba* and her long gorgeous legs got everybody stirred up including Bowles.

"You're not naked," Mili replied. "You've got bubbles covering everything except your breasts, doll. Which, by the way, appear to be defying gravity, unless they're just floating on the water."

Mardie grinned and looked at her sister—blonde, beautiful, blue-eyed Mili. Could have been a young Meryl Streep's twin instead of hers. Mili's Hellion body was lovely, what little she chose to reveal. Like the fat lady of Scotland Yard she used to be, Mili still wore loose slacks and puffy tops. But Mardie suspected that the female structures supporting her blouse were awesome.

"Why don't you strip down and get in here with me?" she asked Mili, grinning wickedly.

"You just want to see my boobs," Mili countered. "I'll tell you straight out. Yours are better."

"Maybe," Mardie admitted. "But I was actually more interested in whose were *bigger*."

"Why don't you just let my double-D cup answer that?" Mili shot back. "Besides, the objects you really should reveal are bubbled over." Mili pointed at the clouds of bath bubbles covering Mardie's front and back.

"Honey, at my age, those things are best hidden from daylight viewing."

"Ha!" Mili chirped.

"Besides," Mardie went on, "with your total body makeover you don't get to vote on how a real ass looks at sixty-eight." Mardie propped up her other leg and spread on shave gel. She noticed a breakout of spider veins near her ankle. "Well, shit," she said irritably, touching the blemishes. "I thought nothing was supposed to change down here. Every time I shave there seem to be more of these bastards."

"Well, not to appear like I'm reminding you *ad infinitum*," Mili chided, "but Lucifer will arrange for *your* redo whenever you decide you're ready."

Mardie glanced at Mili.

"Believe me, I never forget that. It's just that right now I like being my age. I'm not young. And I'm not beautiful. But I'm—" Mardie frowned and struggled to find the right word.

"Ripe?" Mili offered. "Like cheese?"

"Shut up. I'm *full*. I'm developed. I'm completed. *Those* kinds of things. And for whatever reason, that feels really good right now. I don't want to be young with all that goes with that. You, of all the people, should know what that's like after your switcheroo."

"No argument from me," Mili responded. "It's like I've started all over with a husband and a daughter to raise. I'm old, but I'm not old. Makes me feel weird."

"Well, you did sort of do the time-warp dance," Mardie said, focused on shaving her leg. "And like Sarah in that Old Testament reenactment play, you had a baby when you were already—mature."

"I'm not laughing."

Mardie kept working on her leg and thought about her sister's situation. Mili was sixty-eight after all, despite looking like a youthful Hollywood starlet now. Who knew how old Lucifer was? But they had a happy marriage and a little girl they loved. All of Hell had rejoiced when Lucifer returned after his seven-year absence.

And when he showed off his wedding ring, multitudes of Hell's residents had followed suit, choosing by the millions to get hitched, too, giving the huge population of priests and rabbis in Hell something to do for a change. Down here only the born agains normally went to church. But everybody loved a wedding.

Mardie applied a little more gel to her shin and wondered if Mili liked sex. Personally, she still liked sex a lot, although the range of coital options had dialed down to just the missionary position for her and Bowles. Nothing wrong with a little face time. Neither Lucifer nor Mili ever mentioned whether the folks in Heaven did it. Why shouldn't they? Maybe the saints were a little more circumspect. It was Heaven after all, the real origin of "Keep Calm and Carry On." So there probably wasn't a lot of shouting. Unless someone was doing anal.

"You and Lu do it before you got married?" Mardie asked.

Mili's face didn't change.

"Do I look like a stoolie?" she replied.

"I was just curious. I mean, you never got married on Earth. I'm guessing that your sexual experiences may have been limited."

"My," Mili said, clearly amused. "How delicately stated. May I remind you that you never got married either, though I suspect your vagina has deeper grooves than the wagon ruts on the Appian Way."

Mardie roared with delight, dropped her naked leg back into the bath, and splashed water everywhere. Mili kicked off a sandal, put her foot in the tub, and splashed Mardie back.

"How many guys have you slept with, really?" she asked.

Mardie stared at her.

"What?"

"Do you need a calculator?"

Mardie laughed and shook her head.

"I'll tell you if you tell me."

"You're on," Mili replied. "I'll go first as my saga will likely be somewhat more brief than yours."

"It's not like my numbers stack up against Pi," Mardie retorted, "if that's what you're implying. Go ahead."

"I slept with four men," Mili confessed. "One of them was someone else's husband. Our tete-a-tete took place every week for years."

"Tete-a-tete? Is that French for sixty-nine?"

Mili rolled her eyes.

"It's French for being together. He worked for a high-tech company in London. My other trysts were with men at the Yard."

"You slept with men at work?" Mardie was genuinely shocked. "Holy shit. You must have been hornier than I ever imagined."

Mili looked confused.

"That's Yankee for needing sex," Mardie clarified.

"It was a lot more than the sex with the married chap," Mili shared softly. "I am sure I loved him as much as I could have ever loved a husband. I think he felt the same about me."

"But he never left his wife?"

"No. He stayed married. But he never left me, either."

Mardie thought about that. She discovered a bit of thatch on her left thigh that had escaped the blade. She shaved it clean and inspected the blade. The hairs were white. Didn't matter. Stubble was stubble. As intolerable to men as prolonged coitus without an ejaculation.

"Your turn," Mili said.

"I can't really give you a specific roll call like Andie MacDowell in *Four Weddings and a Funeral*," Mardie stated as a caveat. "I would guess a dozen or so in senior school. A few dozen while I was a working stiff. And perhaps a few dozen more up to the point when I didn't have to worry about getting pregnant any more. After that there were dozens and dozens. Since I've been down here probably another dozen and a half."

"Dear God!" Mili exclaimed. "How many men have you had?"

"It's hard to be exact. Last count was 172. Plus or minus." Mardie gazed at Mili. "Are you dismayed?"

"No. I'm flat out jealous. I can't even imagine having all those men to compare to each other."

"You didn't miss much, truth be told," Mardie said. "It's not like there was infinite variation. Most chaps are like cats. They want in. They want out. And about that fast."

"My," Mili whispered, shaking her head. "Did you ever have a climax with any of them?"

"With every one of them," Mardie affirmed. "Mostly when they were snoring afterwards."

Mili giggled.

"I had a lot of those. Without the snoring men."

Mardie laughed so hard waves of water washed over the edge of the tub. She looked at Mili.

"But things are okay for you and Lucifer, right?"

"Yes," Mili answered, happily. "He's tender, never in a hurry, and he lasts forever."

"Now *I'm* jealous. Maybe he could give a couple of pointers to

Bowles. Don't get me wrong. Bowles is wonderful. Just could use a tip or two on the meaning of everlasting."

Mili gasped, then laughed. Mardie stood, grabbed a towel off the rack, and began drying off. She noticed that Mili was checking out her private parts. Actually, more like her private decoration. The hairy seventies were long gone. Mardie shaved her pubic mound bare. She'd done little runways for private landings in the past, and had tried polka dots. But those last ones looked like she'd contracted some outrageous STD. For now, she was shaving it bare. Bowles liked it bare. Mili was frowning. Apparently she didn't like it bare.

"Okay, Mil," Mardie spoke up, "I'm in need of having you move to some other room of the house now."

Mili grabbed her sandals.

"Got any booze?"

"Whatever you like. Some souse in Heaven sends me a case of stuff every week."

Mili grinned.

"Is there any schnapps?"

"There's some of that plum poison you like. What do you call it?"

"Sliwowitz?" Mili asked.

"No. Not the German watered-down stuff. The Serbian one."

"Slivovice," Mili said.

"That's it. Eats your guts right out. A little bit of Hell from Earth. Go pour. I'll be there in two shakes."

"Of?"

"Of my sagging derriere, if you must know."

Mili laughed and went out, shutting the door behind her.

Mardie ran her hand between her legs checking for strays. She found and shaved several on her the mound of Venus. She wanted it perfect because Bowles liked to spend time fooling around down there. Always willing to date a man who did that. Nothing like a good upbringing.

CHAPTER FIVE

I can't really be the only person you can talk to about your worries," Hugh Everett III told Lucifer. The fit and tan young man was dressed in a white T-shirt and blue overalls, and was sitting in a wicker chair on his front porch visiting with Satan who sat in another. The fingers of Everett's right hand were twirling corkscrews in his bushy black beard.

"You *are* the only person, believe me," Lucifer told him. "The stuff happening in Hell is freaking me out." Lucifer had embarked on a trip through folded space to find Everett, who was now a contented husband, father, and farmer on the alternate world where he had remained after the demise of the serial killer he'd shot years ago. He and Lucifer were alone together drinking Budweisers.

"Hell's got some of the best quantum physics guys anywhere," Everett said. "Why not talk to one of them?"

Lucifer shook his head. He picked up his beer and took a slug. He was dressed in khaki pants, a pink Faconnable shirt, and navy-blue Dockers. "The minute I'd talk to any one of them about the changes I've noticed in Hell, everyone would know."

"The old 'walls have ears' thing?"

"Yeah, except the walls are morphed demons."

Everett chuckled.

Lucifer frowned.

"Do you still do that burning bush thing when you get upset?" Hugh asked.

"The burning bush was Jehovah, you pagan," the Devil replied.

"Oh, yes. Sorry."

"And, for the record, yes. I still do that burning *thing* when the occasion allows."

"Which means when you're not around the wife and kid?"

Lucifer wrinkled his forehead and glared at Everett.

"Have another beer," Hugh offered by means of a diversion, taking another cold Budweiser out of the red cooler next to his chair and handing it to the Devil. "Why don't we talk about Edward's Perfect Game?" Everett wagged his head in awe just imaging it. "I really don't know how that barrel of fat can bowl like that.

"I was obese once and I bowled like shit. *And* it should be impossible for *anyone* to bowl The Perfect Game given the physics of Hell. There are immutable, divinely ordained rules that do not allow for an exception like that, ever. Any more than there can be a natural exception to gravity on Earth. Imagine Albert Einstein jumping off a bridge and not smashing into mush. Mother Nature doesn't allow one-offs."

Lucifer stared at Everett surprised. Mother Nature?

Hugh saw it and grinned.

"It's just an expression."

"For morons."

Everett laughed out loud.

"Not to play the Devil's advocate," Lucifer said and cocked his head. "I am under the impression that *some* quantum physicists think that anything is possible, anywhere, anytime."

"Who the hell have you been talking to?" Everett said sarcastically.

"Nobody," Lucifer shot back, but his lie was written all over his face.

"Wayne Dyer?"

The Devil gave Everett a withering look.

"Deepak Chopra?"

Lucifer kept a stone face.

"All right, never mind," Hugh said and chuckled. "The plain truth is that physics is immutable and unforgiving. Between Edward's game and your discovery of the dandelion, the evidence points to only one conclusion—the physics of Hell are changing."

"But you just said that divine physics didn't allow for exceptions," Satan pointed out.

"And that's true enough," Hugh agreed amicably. "But I never said that the physics of a place could not be changed by the one and only Keyholder."

"Are you saying that God is changing Hell's natural laws?"

"I'm only saying that the phenomenon of The Perfect Game *and* a perfect flower is evidence that God is up to something. Furthermore, since these marvels happened back to back, as it were, they may well be harbingers of more to come."

Satan's eyes grew wide.

"More flowers?"

Hugh shrugged.

"Would that really be so bad?"

"Yes, it would!" Lucifer cried offended. "I'm in charge of Hell, not Disneyland!"

Everett arched an eyebrow.

"People like Disneyland," he said.

"Well, they can't have it down there," Satan almost shouted, he was so upset. "They're in Hell for a reason, remember? It's supposed to be hot and dirty, and unpleasant, for God's sake. Not full of flowers."

Hugh shrugged again and took a swallow from his beer bottle.

Lucifer downed the rest of his.

"So what are you going to do?" Everett asked.

37

"All I can do for now is wait," Lucifer admitted, realizing that Hugh's comments had offered him none of the answers he had been hoping for. If Hell's very laws were changing, he'd have to witness what else went wrong before seeking any more advice from Hugh.

"You probably won't have to wait long," Hugh offered by way of commiseration. "Far more significant than The Perfect Game, or the brave dandelion, is that the eternal gray skies over Hell have parted and revealed what has never been seen before. Blue skies. And your sun. That is so momentous, it is likely that you are probably heading for a total upheaval of *everything* in Hell. You might want to consult with Jehovah."

Hugh shrugged seeing Satan's disappointment.

"Best advice I can offer."

Lucifer knew that what was happening in Hell matched *exactly* what God liked to do. Planting clues about what He was up to that presaged mighty changes ahead. His obtuse hints about the identity and deeds of the Messiah sprinkled throughout the Old Testament had spawned a worldwide industry of apostles, clergy, and television evangelists all trying to apply them to Jesus.

Others of Jehovah's prophetic tidbits were mystifying and problematic. Very possibly because they weren't his at all, though they had been accepted as such. The author of the Biblical *Book of Revelation* boldly proclaimed that only 144,000 people were going to Heaven. So once the city of Spokane was saved, everyone else was out of luck. That presaged big gains for Hell though, now that he thought about it. Such supposedly inspired prophecies were taken very seriously by hardline Bible scholars and lay people alike. Sometimes opposing interpretations had even caused conflict and bloodshed between Christians.

Lucifer remembered being delighted and astonished when Christian Greeks engaged in a civil war in the nineteenth century, killing each other over whether a believer should use two or three fingers to make the sign of the cross. It was really too bad that Jesus had risen from the dead. Lucifer would have loved to see him spinning in his grave over that one.

The Devil didn't ordinarily deal with Muslims, but their straightforward interpretations of God's motivations based on the Qur'an sparked some interesting Islamic dogmas. His hands-down favorite was the strange and rather outrageous belief that Allah had promised true Islamic martyrs an entry into Paradise sweetened by the welcome of seventy-two virgins who would be their exclusive property.

My. What was God thinking? One virgin was boring beyond belief. He couldn't even begin to fathom scores of them waiting their turn. How did a martyr handle such a thing? His own choice of a harem would be composed of the girls in Hell who'd turned tens of thousands of tricks. He was sure they could turn his trick a time or two.

He looked at Hugh.

Hugh gazed back at him.

"How are things in this new world?" Satan asked, changing the subject. "For you?"

Everett blinked, surprised. The Devil had never asked him one single question before except for 'Do you think you can get us out of here?' some twenty years ago.

"It's fine," Everett told him.

"You're not experiencing issues being a Hellion on a duplicate Earth?"

"Not yet. The Hellion body you secured for me is the right age for my wife and family. Years from now I'll start to stick out though."

Satan nodded.

"You can always come back to Hell—" The Devil paused and phrased his words carefully.

"—when things here change."

"Or I can stay here and reinvent myself, " Everett mused.

Lucifer finished his beer.

"Another one?" Everett asked.

Satan nodded, trading his empty for the cold one that Hugh handed him.

"You're smart enough to figure out how to 'reincarnate' without being discovered," the Devil agreed. "It's harder to do than you might think, but some folks have done it successfully. Even on Earth."

"Dick Cheney?" Hugh guessed.

Lucifer was impressed and his face showed it.

"How did you know?"

"I didn't really. Just ran through the probabilities. There always seems to be a guy like that around, advising well-intentioned, but weak-willed men. A few such characters in that mold even *look* like Cheney—rotund, bald, beady-eyed. Otto Bismarck. Hermann Goring. Joe McCarthy—"

"Okay, already," Lucifer interrupted. "Who else have you guessed?"

"Some genuine do-gooders."

"Such as?"

"Frederick Douglas. Aka Washington Carver. Aka Nelson Mandela."

"Man, you *are* good," the Devil granted Hugh, impressed. "Why don't we see just how good?"

Everett nodded grinning.

"A later incarnation of Pompey?"

"Ataturk."

"Queen of Sheba?"

"Rosa Parks."

"Cassius?"

"John Wilkes Booth."

"You are *damn* good, sir." Satan raised his hand and saluted Hugh with genuine admiration. "Any one you're not sure of?"

"Khufu?" Hugh asked, naming the builder of the first Giza pyramid. No image had survived of him save a two-inch ivory portrait. Even his mummified body had been lost. Had that been deliberate?

"Eva Peron," the Devil answered instantly.

"Ho, ho!" Everett cried out. "I knew she was too good to be true. And *her* mummified body went missing too!"

"Well, what do you think about that?" Satan answered, eyes twinkling.

"May I ask about another possible Hellion?"

"As many as you like," Lucifer said obligingly.

"Aristotle?"

"Think Stephen Hawking."

"Of course," Hugh murmured.

"Cleopatra?"

"Martha Stewart."

"No! Really?"

"She's into cooking and decorating this particular time around. Cleo's body is missing, too, remember?"

"I thought I heard that she was in Hell."

"Only visiting," Lucifer clarified. "Checking on business actually. She's got a monopoly on white wine imports."

"How about Alexander the Great?"

"Tom Custer."

"You mean *George* Custer."

"No, Tom Custer." Satan smiled, pleased at Hugh's mistake. "Two-time Congressional Medal of Honor winner. The first soldier to be so decorated. Died at Little Big Horn with his older brother. Body never identified."

"Awesome."

"Truly. If all these folks could all pull off a succession of multiple identities, then there's no reason why a brilliant man like you shouldn't be able to do it."

"Well, thank you," Everett said gratefully. "I know it's a ways off, but I am encouraged to think that when I have to move on, I will indeed be able to do so."

"You're welcome," Lucifer said, and stood. "Time for me to go."

Everett stood up and shook Satan's hand.

"Good luck on your problem," he said sincerely. His face turned inquisitive, stamped with yearning. "One more guess for the road?"

Lucifer smiled obligingly.

"Make it as tough as you can," he dared Everett.

Hugh jumped at the opportunity knowing instantly who he wanted to ask about.

"Justinian and Theodora?" he blurted out, naming the greatest Byzantine emperor and his ambitious wife.

Satan went tsk, tsk, tsk, mocking Everett's choice.

"You actually think that a pair of Hellions could have teamed up *and* managed to fool the entire world, over and over again?"

"Damned straight I do," Everett said.

Lucifer smiled indulgently.

"I love your big brain," he said. "Their current incarnations are Bill and Hillary Clinton."

"You are the man!" Hugh cried.

Lucifer grinned.

"Archangel actually."

Everett high-fived the Devil who slapped his hand with a loud smack, then waved and headed off for home, the onetime Prince of Heaven whom no one had imitated in the past, and whom none would dare imitate in the future. There might be a Triune God, but there was only one Satan.

CHAPTER SIX

Hell got back to normal quickly. The clouds moved back together to block out every ray of sun. The sidewalks of New Babylon failed to generate any more dandelions. It was hot. It was dirty. It was Hell.

Lucifer sipped on a sugary raspberry lemonade at the gallery bar inside the uber-air-conditioned Avalon Lanes. Preparation for the last semifinal round of the championship bowling tournament was in high gear, and he was taking refreshment before the next bowling teams showed up.

He had enjoyed visiting with Hugh Everett III, though their conversation hadn't really provided any definitive explanations as to why random good things were happening down here. After the series of murders in Hell a few years ago, things had settled down into the same predictably sour and uncomfortable routines that made Hell, hell. But now for the first time since the serial killer's appearance years ago, damnation was going awry. He used to feel like the master of this foul place. Now he was feeling like a jailer whose facility was falling apart.

Strictly speaking, Lucifer was well aware that he had neither power *in* nor control *of* Hell. His position was that of a figurehead acting as a steward for Jehovah. But God never came here, and things had gone on so predictably for so long without Him that Lucifer had learned to enjoy the illusion that he was in charge. Which, plain and simple, *was* an illusion. Just pretend. Like Peter Pan and Neverland. The humbling fact was that Hell's garbage men were considerably more important to perdition's welfare than Lucifer, though he did get to wear nicer clothes than they did. And he got to hang out here at Avalon Lanes.

He looked around with a sense of contentment. The bowling alley was a constant respite from the reality of Hell, though he never considered it a place of refuge from Mili or Little Mardie. Also, unknown to everyone except himself and his wife, they were actively trying to have another child. God had a son. Why not him? Lu, Jr. Someone to bowl with.

Satan glanced at the clock hanging over the bar. It was one fifteen. Forty-five minutes until the start of the second semifinal. The British Royals had advanced to the final with their victory over The American Presidents. That had been a classic series between two very civilized teams. The same would not be said of today's competitors, The European Dictators and The African Dictators. Both squads had histories of yelling, cursing, name-calling, and dismemberment.

The European team entered the alley wearing orange silk athletic pant suits with *Euro Dics* embroidered in green across their shoulders. They were followed by the African team wearing black linen shirts and skirts. Sewn in black on the backs of their shirts was The Potentates. Of course, no one could read the black-on-black team name. Any comments were brushed off by The African Dictators saying, they knew who they were. Indeed. And *we* all know what you did when you were alive, Satan thought. Not the brightest sons of Hell, but some of the most deserving of being here. Welcome, boys.

The African team gathered at their bench, laced up their shoes, powdered their hands, and prepared to bowl some practice frames. Lucifer watched the team captain, Idi Amin of Uganda. He had had the audacity to have his titles embroidered in red on the front of his shirt as well: His Excellency, President for Life, Field Marshall Al Hadji Doctor Idi Amin, VC, DSO, MC, Lord of the Beasts of the Earth and Fishes of the Sea, and Conqueror of the British Empire in Africa in General, and Uganda in Particular.

The man was a huge tub of lard with a brain apparently made of the same material. Lord of the Beasts of the Earth and Fishes of the Sea? Egad. Yet for all his lunacy, Amin was a great bowler, having led his team to the postseason championship rounds every year since he had first arrived down here. And his teams had won the title more than ten times. He was a force to be reckoned with.

Amin noticed Lucifer looking at him. Neither acknowledged the other. Neither liked the other. Satan was sure that if Amin was offered any opportunity to own a working freezer, the former dictator would spare no effort to arrange to have the Devil's head cut off and stored in it for his viewing pleasure.

Joseph Mobutu arrived, the psychopath who had ruled Zaire for thirty years. He'd managed to loot more money from his subjects than bloody Leopold of Belgium had done when it was still called the Congo. Mobutu nodded respectfully toward Lucifer. A gentleman despite his flaws. Satan nodded back. The man was probably the richest soul down here, with the exception of himself. Mobutu had been bribing demons for decades into making withdrawals from his Swiss bank accounts and delivering the francs. The evil that men do lives after them, and with careful planning so does their money.

And speaking of evil, Satan gazed at Jean-Bedel Bokassa, the self-declared royal who had reigned over the Central African Republic. He was truly as wicked and murderous as any of history's genuine royals. He was also a self-confessed cannibal. He joined his team leading a procession of toadies carting his shoes, gloves, bowling balls, and God knew what kinds of refreshments in three portable ice coolers.

The last member of The Potentates foursome was recent arrival Muammar Gaddafi, a five-star dictator by anyone's standards. He had siphoned off billions of dollars from Libyan oil revenues over the course of his decades of rule. He had also jailed, raped, and murdered thousands of unfortunates from among his six million subjects. As a self-confessed Muslim, Muammar should actually have gone to Muslim Hell. But the fact was he was an atheist and had been sent to join that exclusive club down here.

Lucifer looked over at the two Samn judges stationed on either side of his judge's stool. Built like the Hellboy comic figure, they looked like Mafia Wiseguys on steroids. They were, in fact, Central Asian demigods packing fire power on a par with Heaven's Archangels.

Samns liked tearing things apart. Especially human bodies. The African bowlers stared at the Samns with fear in their eyes. Be good lads and you haven't got anything to worry about, Satan thought. Mobutu, Bokassa, and Gaddafi nodded their heads respectfully toward the Devil. Idi Amin raised his hand and gave Lucifer the finger. Ah, Satan thought, one can try and conceal it, but true sportsmanship will always win out.

Lucifer briefly considered having Amin's hand chopped off. But the dictator needed it for more than just bowling. Idi and his teammates had day jobs picking up street litter and dog duty, piece by piece, without shovels. And without gloves. Some people really did get punished in Hell. Oh, not the fire and brimstone thing, but hard labor, with no days off—not even Christmas—unless they made the bowling championships.

Lucifer walked up to Idi Amin and spoke to him just loud enough for him to hear.

"I'll make sure that whatever dogs roam Hell are encouraged by my people to shit on the streets you clean the next few weeks."

Amin stared at him.

The Devil smiled. Hopefully there would be some Great Danes and Saint Bernard's in that number. He turned his attention to The European Dictators.

Benito Mussolini managed to somehow look like he was swaggering even while standing still. He postured as though he was still Italy's Fascist Supreme. The only aspect that diminished his earnest affectation were the countless bullet holes in his face and hands—and as well all the rest of his body parts—compliments of Italian partisans after his capture. Carrying Mussolini's sport bag was Adolf Hitler. He was wearing jeans and a white T-shirt. Der Former Fuhrer was actually an excellent bowler himself, but the Jews in Hell had petitioned that he not be allowed to compete and the Devil had honored that.

Shuffling in and hoping to be more or less ignored was Ante Pavelic. The infamous Croatian dictator, assassin, and Nazi puppet had tried to murder every non-Catholic in his country. He saw Lucifer and quickly looked away. In life, Pavelic had ordered the torture, dismemberment, and murder of hundreds of thousands of Serb Muslims and Jews. He had their eyeballs removed and stored in huge jars in his office. In Hell, Satan required that he eat eyeballs at every meal supplied to him directly from Earth's mortuaries.

He wasn't required to dine alone, however. He was usually joined by Eugenio Maria Giuseppe Giovanni Pacelli, aka Pope Pius XII, who had hidden him from the victorious allies at the end of World War II. From there he arranged to have him smuggled out of Rome to Argentina, where Pavelic lent his considerable genocidal talents to Juan Peron.

For these and other pious deeds as pope, Eugenio had been declared a *Servant of God* by Pope John Paul II. Pope Benedict XVI had followed by honoring him with the title *Venerable*. Those official spiritual elevations placed Eugenio securely on the path to sainthood. And why not, Lucifer thought? Saints were often made of malevolent stuffing. His own favorite saints were Hernan Cortes and Francisco Pizarro. Well, at least *he* would have made them saints.

The third Euro Dic team member was once the absolute dictator of Spain, Francisco Franco. The Devil couldn't stand being around the tall, bony Spaniard. Not because of his crimes—though he got credited for an almost infinite number—but for his incredible stupidity and dullness. The man couldn't add up two pesetas, yet he had somehow managed to climb to the top of the military oligarchy that had overthrown Spain's royal government. He had then governed as dictator for almost forty years.

Franco was emptying his sport bag and avoiding eye contact with his team members lest he see someone whose name he would not be able to remember. No one on the team greeted him. Mussolini couldn't, because he'd been shot through the jaw. And Pavelic refused, holding him in contempt for allowing the Spanish Catholic Church to devolve into a weak and wasted institution, while Spaniards ate, drank, divorced, and got abortions.

The last and final member of The European Dictator's bowling team strutted in late. He was short and burly with an erect carriage, a handsome head of thick, graying hair, and a rugged, beat-up face that would have been a badge of honor for any boxer. Waving happily to his team, Joseph Stalin hummed an old Georgian folk tune while he unpacked his bowling essentials from the large, belted, wicker suitcase he had carried into the alley. Satan nodded when Stalin spotted him. The Marxist leader bowed deeply.

Known for his ruthless domination of Communist Russia and responsibility for the starvation of millions of its people because of his daft collective farming edict, Joe was only rarely remembered as a seminary student who'd gotten himself kicked out of divinity school for reading banned political books long before he helped mastermind the Russian Revolutions of 1905 and 1917. Vladimir Lenin had been absolutely terrified of him before the rest of his advisors realized how soulless Stalin was. When they did, everyone in Lenin's inner circle worked tirelessly to assassinate him.

Instead, what was planned for the goose, happened to the gander. Stalin smothered Lenin with his own bed pillow. Stalin had been the best dictator Lucifer had ever seen. A dictator's dictator. He not only massacred minorities and Jews, but also his own countrymen as well. Top Communist leaders and every Soviet general who had ever won a battle were executed, on the off chance that they might be eyeing Stalin's job.

In another life he would have made a ferocious Homeland Security head, or even better, a dependable and worthy successor to Dick Cheney. Vice President Stalin never would have made it to the presidency though, as he would likely have killed off his campaign managers and a goodly number of his supporters, too.

Lucifer surveyed both teams of men—monsters really—their vast and shameless crimes rendering completely petty all the other sins like adultery, theft, and accidental homicide that had landed most of the rest of the damned population down here. It was a wonder that God hadn't torn the eight members of these two bowling teams to pieces for their crimes. Of course, Satan knew that he was not one to judge what the Almighty should and shouldn't do. He had, after all, once upon a time tried to kill God.

Maybe he should start his own bowling team. Problem was, he'd likely be limited to Biblical villains, the likes of Pontius Pilate, Joseph Caiaphas, and Herod the Great. And none of them could bowl worth shit.

CHAPTER SEVEN

The Wickett sisters were sitting at Mardie's wonderful kitchen table with its dazzling marquetry surface of inlaid woods, drinking tea and eating butter cookies. Actually, Mardie was just drinking tea, but Mili was eating cookies stamped with Queen Elizabeth's portrait, celebrating her sixtieth anniversary on the throne. And washing them down with *her* tea.

Mardie sat barefoot with her legs crossed, dressed in a pink terrycloth bathrobe, looking a bit haggard. Mili had on white retro pedal pushers, a sleeveless, fuchsia cotton top, and silver sandals. She looked fresh and chipper. It hurt Mardie's eyes to look at her.

"What's wrong with your voice?" Mili asked her.

"I'm a bit hoarse," Mardie said, "that's all."

"You're a *lot* hoarse," Mili corrected her. "Do a bit of hollering at the bowling championships?"

"Not on your life," Mardie croaked. "Those bowlers are the worst of the worst evil doers."

"*Worst* evil doers?" Mili asked. "Wickedness is relative and therefore hard to scale."

Mardie stared at her twin, convinced she couldn't be serious.

"Nicking a stick of your friend's gum versus murdering him for a quid from his wallet is *relative*?" she asked Mili, sounding quite irritable. "The bastards bowling in the league playoffs are mass murderers, far beyond any *relative* comparison to anyone else except each other."

"Again, there are mass murderers," Mili said, "and there are mass murderers."

Mardie stared at her sister.

"Just shut up," she snapped.

Mili grinned.

"So tell me about the hoarse voice."

"I had a late night."

"That involved a lot of hollering?"

"More along the lines of gasping and squealing."

Mardie frowned.

"Oh, my God," she murmured.

"Want to know more?"

"Not unless you were with one of the bowlers."

Mardie grimaced.

"Oh, please. How can you stand that game let alone the assholes who play it?"

"I only watch the championships. The American Presidents were eliminated yesterday by The British Royals, and the Brits will face the winner of today's other semifinal. The African Potentates or The European Dictators. Though The Potentates were almost disqualified during their quarterfinal match against The Filipino Dictators."

"I heard that Idi Amin stuck it to Ferdinand Marcos."

Mili snorted and grabbed a handful of butter cookies.

"He actually stuck a knife in Imelda Marcos' butt."

"What?" Mardie cried, and grimaced just imagining it.

"Mrs. Marcos had just berated him for shouldering her husband on his way to the lane and Amin pulled out a concealed dagger and popped it in her tush when she turned her back on him."

"And that wasn't enough to get The Potentates kicked out of the tournament?"

"No. Imelda pulled it out and stuck it in one of Idi's eyes."

Mardie cringed.

"And what happened to Mrs. Marcos? I don't recall hearing that she's joined her husband down here."

"She hasn't. She's still alive," Mili revealed. "She bribed her way down here to see the qualifying matches for the championship."

"How could she even know that they were going on?"

"Same way anyone else on Earth finds out stuff. She used a medium."

Mardie shook her head and laughed. Her voice cracked, unpleasantly. She coughed, then shook her head again.

"I never thought any of those charlatans knew anything."

"It depends on their connections with the demon network," Mili explained. "And, of course, on precisely what questions they are asked."

"You mean, like, is my husband Ferdinand happy in the afterlife?"

"Precisely. Whatever the psychic answers, it's based on data gathered by devils."

"My," Mardie said. "Why not just eliminate all those middle men and plug this place into Facebook?"

"That's not going to happen," Mili replied. "Jehovah will never allow formal communications between Earth and Hell."

"Then what about just for the people down here then?"

"*That* we might be able to do," Mili answered. "We could call it *Friedbook*."

Despite her hoarseness Mardie barked out a sharp laugh. Then she reached for her tea cup and gulped down a few swallows.

"So despite Imelda and Idi's brouhaha," Mili continued, "The Potentates remained in the championships and Mrs. Marcos was escorted out of the bowling alley. She was sent to Earth using the hole by the bar. Word came back that she bitched because it dumped her in San Francisco."

"I'm sure she managed to make the best of it," Mardie commented. "Isn't there a Bloomingdale's there?"

Mili nodded.

"And Saks Fifth Avenue, Neiman Marcus, Barney's, Bottega Venega, and Dior—and there are more places that *just* carry shoes."

"Oh, yeah," Mardie deadpanned. "Shoes. One can never have too many shoes."

"But one can attempt to."

Both sisters laughed.

✳ ✳ ✳

Despite the air conditioning being dialed up to hurricane force, Avalon Lanes bowling alley was hot. It was packed with fans there to witness the semifinal competition between The European Dictators and The African Dictators, though everyone was interested in getting a glimpse at Lucifer as well.

The Lord of Hell was standing at the gallery bar sipping on a lemonade. No one waved, winked, or shouted out a greeting. But everyone watched him. Little really was known about the somewhat cloaked activities of the Prince of Darkness. There were rumors that he saw God. That he was married. That he had an heir to the throne. There had even been rumors that someone had tried to kill him, but those had never been confirmed. Demons told stories about bodies showing up at his house, but as far as anyone knew, those poor unfortunate souls might have simply gone afoul of Satan himself and paid the price.

Lucifer saw the hundreds of pairs of eyes watching him. The price of fame. No, that wasn't quite right. The price of infamy? Nope, not right either. He picked up his lemonade and took a sip. Ah, he had it. The price of Hellfamy.

He reached for his handkerchief and dabbed at his forehead. He was perspiring heavily. Whether due to the full house or his third sugary lemonade, he didn't know. He had his black-and-white striped judge's shirt. He didn't need to wear it to officiate at the bowling games, but why not? He was the only bowling judge in Hell.

The heat was also getting to Idi Amin. Wearing a new black eye patch, he was sweating profusely, drops trailing down his fat cheeks. He was scooping them up with a fingertip and flinging them over the ball return at The Euro Dics. To their credit they were ignoring him, displaying their trademark European cool which, as it always had, continued to make the African dictator both irritable and envious.

Satan looked around the gallery. He didn't see Mili anywhere, nor their daughter. His sister-in-law Mardie was missing also, but that didn't surprise him too much. She'd often told him that unless the players were throwing their own balls down the alleys, she had very little interest in how the sport was played.

He noticed that Teddy Roosevelt and his daughter Alice were sitting in the front row of the gallery. Teddy had been a New York City police commissioner, a US president, and a big game hunter. He'd gone for the kill in each one of those pursuits. And then there was Alice, still with a creamy smooth face at age ninety-six thanks to Hell's top plastic surgeons. Despite the tomfoolery performed on her face, she was forced to occupy her ancient, bone-thin body. Teddy was smoking a cigar. Alice was eating popcorn. It wouldn't have surprised Satan if the two had switched activities.

Little Mardie loved Alice and very likely was the only person who did besides Teddy. The woman was absolutely scathing with her comments, always sour and perverse, and unsurpassed for sheer orneriness. Even Lucifer avoided her. The last time she'd seen him, he'd been wearing a tuxedo for a roasting of Philip Roth. She'd looked him up and down and remarked that if there was such a thing as a divorce cake he could be the little ex-groom on the top. Never mind that her stinging comment was only a recycled version of her wicked take on Al Smith running for president back when. It pissed Satan off. Divorce cake, indeed.

Lucifer walked toward the judge's high stool. The crowd realized why he was heading there and erupted in cheers. He liked that noise. Made you feel happy, no matter who was doing it. There weren't many things were like that. Smiles. Laughter. Porn.

Satan lifted his arms to address the crowd.

"Ladies and gentlemen," he said. "Welcome to the last semifinal. The winner will advance to the final to face The British Royals who won their match yesterday against The American Presidents. Please welcome The African Dictators and The European Dictators."

The bowling alley went mad. There were great cheers and vicious curses giving a rich festiveness to the atmosphere. The Potentates pumped their fists in the air during the raucous display. The Euro Dics waved benignly, displaying the preternatural calm of a twenty-term parliament member who'd just been reelected again.

Lucifer's introduction turned out to be about the most exciting moment of the game. Both teams played well, but failed to display anything anyone hadn't seen a thousand times before—this strike, that spare, good scores, but nothing approaching The Perfect Game. After the first series, there was a break for the players to rest, and for the fans to eat and drink. Lucifer walked over to say hello to Teddy and Alice Roosevelt. He'd have preferred to chat with Mili and Little Mardie, but they still hadn't shown up.

Mili loved The British Royals and had watched her team wind its way through preliminary rounds, including their victories over The Apostate Maya, Hugh Hefner's Playmates of the Year, and The Salem Witch Trial Judges, to make it all the way to the final. Satan thought Apostate sounded a bit judgmental, but considering the Maya had eliminated the Jesuits he had to consider it an in-your-face team name.

On the other hand, the Playmates' name sort of said it all, and each year he had to regretfully turn down the team's request to play in the nude, citing it as an unfair advantage over their opponents. Every year they appealed his decision, claiming that they played better in the nude. Satan had no doubt that was true. Turned them down anyway. He also believed that granting their request might result in antics that would cheapen a noble sport. From his vantage point the game had barely survived American television's Bowling for Dollars.

"Hello, Teddy," the Devil greeted the famous president, and received a bone-crushing handshake from the former Rough Rider. More like Rough Handshaker. He dutifully leaned forward to collect a dry kiss on his cheek from Roosevelt's daughter, Alice. Down here, Alice was some twenty-five years older than her father. Yeah, yeah. So what? This was Hell and that's how old they'd been when they'd arrived.

Alice's face was thin and rouged, her blue eyes staggeringly aggressive, and her dyed-blonde hair twisted into a bun on the top of her head. Teddy's face looked as though he'd been punched into a likeness of the Venus of Willendorf—plump, pasty, and ugly. Roosevelt had never been a handsome man, but now the poor chap's face was only fit for the front pages of tabloids who'd claim that he'd been beaten up by an unknown evil adversary. Alice perhaps. His thick, salt-and-pepper hair was slicked back with rose water, and he was wearing an amber-lensed Ray Ban pince-nez.

As hot as it was, the president was wearing a brown wool suit with a vest. Alice had on an almost sheer blue-and-white floor-length gown. Lucifer was sorry that Little Mardie wasn't here to see it. His daughter was head over heels in love with Alice's wardrobe of blue gowns, all feminine, all elegant, all designed when she had been young and beautiful. Those days were gone, but Satan had to admit that the old bag had had taste.

The Devil noticed that Teddy was holding a handful of double eagle gold pieces, shiny and inviting. He glanced at Alice. She had a stack of the same big coins balanced on her leg.

"Are you and your daughter wagering?" he asked Roosevelt, mock disapproval in his voice.

"Guilty as charged, my dear sir," Roosevelt answered.

"Who do you favor between these two sets of bullies today?" Alice interrupted, looking Lucifer square in the face. It struck the Devil that the dowager always seemed to be somehow trying to master his will with her gaze. There was nothing coy, or flirtatious, or for that matter, subtle about her effort to dominate his mind. Lucifer felt like he had been snared by the gaze of Medusa.

"I don't wager," he replied, pulling free of the terrific force of her trance. "I wouldn't know how to pick one team over another."

Alice scowled at him as though he were giving her the brush-off.

God, the woman could read minds.

"I can do your job," she said menacingly.

"I bet you can," the Devil replied. "Maybe better than me."

"I am serious," Alice almost hissed.

"I've never seen you when you were not, even with your penchant for sarcastic barbs."

A small smile crept across Alice's thin lips.

"You are a charmer, Lucifer. Too bad I'm not a little younger, and you a little more infatuated with sex."

Lucifer looked surprised. Was Alice baiting him? Flirting with him? What a woman. If he got too close, she'd probably eat him up in a single bite. He smiled at her, bowed his head ever so slightly, and went back to his judge's stool. He'd never met anyone like her. If and when he would ever have to be absent from Hell again for any duration, he'd ban the Demon Council from reforming and just hand things over to Alice. That woman was made of sterner stuff than he. Closer on the periodic table to asbestos. Jehovah didn't know how lucky he and the saints were that she'd wound up down here.

A rumble ran through the massive crowd as word spread that Lucifer was heading back to his seat. The European Dictators were inspecting the alley, the ball return, and their own prize bowling balls. They were also checking out the floor beneath the team bench for bombs. Old habits die hard.

The Potentates were already seated on their team bench consuming miniature whiskeys, boxes of chocolates, fistfuls of chewing tobaccos, and in Jean-Bedel Bokassa's case, heroin. Satan watched him inject his arm. He could care less what Bokassa or any other of the bad boys used. Whatever enhanced their performance was just fine with him.

"Find out what kind of whiskey General Ulysses Grant drinks," Lincoln had once famously told those who complained about the officer's prodigious alcohol consumption, "and send a barrel of it to each of the rest of my generals." Lucifer smiled happily. God damn, he wished he could have gotten Lincoln down here. Never a real Christian *and* a clandestine homosexual as a young man, Lucifer had watched him lie and cheat and fool his friends, charting a course straight to damnation.

Becoming a rich railroad lawyer seemed to guarantee his fate, and going into politics sealed it. Until the war. Until Lincoln had to *deal* with the war. The deaths of tens of thousands of young men, and the increasingly barbaric treatment of Black people in the South deepened him, and then changed him. A different man emerged inside the White House than the man who had moved into it in 1861.

Lincoln's armies defeated the Confederacy and he wrangled Congress into freeing the slaves, then rose to highest spiritual state a man could aspire by forgiving his enemies and offering them peace. He got himself killed for it, but found himself embraced by Jehovah. The saintliness of the man had become so great it even brought his wife and all of his sons to Heaven as well.

Lucifer shrugged regretfully, then gazed at The European Dictators and The Potentates. They were the flip sides of Lincoln—selfish, egotistical, misogynist, racist, murderous sons of bitches. But could they bowl.

"Gentlemen," Lucifer told them, "let us begin." The bowling alley erupted in prolonged cheering. The Devil smiled and waved to the crowd. There wasn't a Lincoln among them, but every one of them belonged to him. Love the ones you're with.

CHAPTER EIGHT

"W here's Aunt Mardie?" Mili asked her daughter. "We're late for the game."

Mili had on white shorts, a pink halter top, and white sandals with big faux jewels glued to the leather. Little Mardie leaned against the big iron stove in her aunt's kitchen and looked at her mother. She had on her Alice Blue Dress with white lace at the neck, the hem, and the tips of her short sleeves. She wore white cotton socks and black patent leather shoes with straps. A cloth belt with a bow tied in the back secured her waist, but Little Mardie wore a black patent leather belt over it that matched her shoes.

"Aunt Mardie is in the bathroom," she told her mother. Her tone was as limp as her posture. "Do we really have to go, Mom?"

"Your father is expecting us, so what do you think the answer is?"

"But the game already started, Mom," Little Mardie whined, "and there won't be any place to sit, except far away."

"Didn't Alice Roosevelt say she was going to save us seats?"

"You didn't tell me," Little Mardie whined. "Did she actually *promise* to save us places?"

Mili frowned, trying to remember exactly what Alice had said.

61

"Alice did not, in fact, promise to save us seats," she admitted.

"Then we don't have to go?"

"We still have to go."

Mardie walked into the kitchen, tucking her blouse into her jeans. She looked at Mili.

"No reason Little Mardie can't just stay with me," she said.

Mili glared at her sister.

"*You* don't have to go," she told her. "But your niece does."

"Hardly seems fair."

"It's called honoring her father," Mili snapped, and locked eyes with her twin. "Don't make me say more."

Mardie instantly backed down. She looked at Little Mardie whose hopes were about to be dashed.

"She's right, pumpkin," she said simply. Little Mardie instantly looked devastated. "There are times when you do something, even if you don't want to, because it makes your parents happy. Imagine how sad your poor old dad is right now, searching the gallery for your pretty face and not seeing you there. He loves you so much."

Big tears rolled down Little Mardie's cheeks. She loved her father and hurting him was something she would never willingly do. Nonetheless, as she wiped away her tears, she promised herself that her father would not only hear all about her sacrifice, but would get an earful as well about how she felt about being dragged to yet another bowling game.

Mili watched her daughter, wanting so much to hug her, but realized that Little Mardie needed to get past this disappointment on her own. She was old enough at thirteen to know that accepting comfort from the very person who was making you unhappy was just an additional humiliation.

Mili's mobile phone rang. She fished it out of her purse. She glanced at the caller ID. Not a lot of people had her private number. It was Pfotenhauer. She answered. Pfot's face appeared on the small iPhone screen.

"Dear boy," Mili greeted him. "How are you?"

Pfotenhauer smiled shyly. The kindness that both Wickett sisters showed him never failed to make him blush.

"I'm fine, Mrs. Mili. Thanks so much for enquiring."

Pfot smiled, which on his skeletal octogenarian face was a bit of a fright. Mili had read once that many elderly people lost tissue mass in their faces, leaving wrinkled, sinking skin that covered the skull structure with little support or shape. Bingo. Poor Pfot looked like a walking advert for Halloween superstores selling fright masks. The good news was that he would never look any worse down here, the eternal afterworld. The bad news was, of course, that he wouldn't ever look any better, either.

"Is Little Mardie nearby?" Pfotenhauer asked in a quiet voice.

"Yes," Mili answered.

"Then may I suggest that you find a place away from her where I can share some unpleasant news."

"Of course. Hold on a moment."

Mili's heart raced, dreading whatever Pfot had to share. She walked into Mardie's bedroom.

"Pfot, are you still there?"

"I am, indeed, ma'am."

"I'm all alone. Is Lucifer all right?"

"Oh, absolutely, Mrs. Mili, and I am sorry that I didn't just say that right out. My news is about a sad event in Shanty Town."

Mili's immediate thought was that Shanty Town was always chalk full of sad events. The ghetto held tens of millions of Hell's poorest residents. It was the worst part of Hell. The worst place with the worst conditions. And yet, very much like ghettos on Earth, it wasn't populated by the worst people. Just the poorest.

"So what happened in Shanty Town, Pfot?" Mili asked.

"Well, to be precise," Pfot answered, "the incident took place *near* Shanty Town, in an agricultural cooperative."

"One of the places that struggles to produce food down here," Mili commented.

"Yes. There are a lot of cooperatives, all trying to grow basic food-stuffs for Hell's markets. While the results are substandard compared to Earth, the farmers manage to scratch out a living.

A young woman living in a co-op located beyond Shanty Town has gone to its governing board and lodged a serious complaint. She claims that she was sexually assaulted by someone from Shanty Town and wants the individual punished."

"How old is she?" Mili asked.

"Fifteen."

Mili flinched.

"What is she doing in Hell?"

"I'm told that she robbed and murdered aristocrats during the French Revolution. Scalped them, too, and wore their pelts tied to her belt. She was caught and hung when she was fifteen, having pinched royal purses and slit Catholic throats since she was eight."

"My God. And her parents?"

"Apparently trained her before being captured and hung themselves."

Mili shook her head. Good had made the rounds. With evil, there was always something new.

"Too bad her mother wasn't Therese Defarge," she told Pfotenhauer. "She could have been knitting instead of slitting."

"Pardon me?" Pfot was stumped by Mili's reference.

"Never mind, lad," she told him. "The bloody character was fictional anyway. When you use the word *molest*, Pfot, how weighted is that term?"

"If by weighted, you mean how serious, then very, would be my take."

"Go on."

"The woman—"

"How substantial a person is this fifteen-year-old?" Mili interrupted.

"She is described as under five-foot-tall and weighing some forty kilos."

"Then the *woman* is a girl," Mili said, grit in her tone.

"The victim claims that she was approached from behind while working in a co-op orchard, grabbed by the waist and thrown to the ground. When her assailant tried to pull her knickers down she stabbed him in the leg. He screamed and fell, whereupon she stabbed him in the chest. He struggled to his feet and ran off."

"So no sexual congress?"

"Only attempted."

"I don't recall ever hearing of an attempted rape in Hell before."

"Very true, Mum," Pfotenhauer agreed. "There is not a single known episode down here."

"Why not, do you suppose?" Mili asked. "There isn't any judicial system in Hell."

"It is the master's doing," Pfot was quick to reply. "There's no prison and no capital punishment, but there is torture and maiming."

Mili frowned.

"Repeat that."

"Lucifer has always warned residents down here that his code of justice allows a tooth for a tooth and an eye for an eye for those who have been hurt by anyone else. It is a powerful deterrent because whatever damage is meted out to the offender's body lasts forever and ever."

"Examples?"

Pfot shrugged and shook his head.

"Ma'am, there just aren't any."

It was a very primitive deterrence, Mili thought critically, but apparently effective. Until now. Some miscreant had tried to have his way with a mite of a girl in a distant orchard. Perhaps he should have chosen his prey a bit more carefully. The one he had attacked stabbed him to the quick. Judging by her history, he was lucky he didn't get his scalp peeled off.

"Where is the girl now?" Mili asked.

"She is being observed in the kibbutz infirmary."

Mili almost dropped her phone.

"Where?"

"The co-operative's infirmary."

"You said kibbutz."

"Same thing."

"Not really, my dear Pfot. Hippies run co-ops. Jews run kibbutzes."

"The person who called me about the incident called it a kibbutz. Sorry I didn't think to specify that earlier."

"Who, by the way, was the person who called you? And why you?"

"It actually was a demon. A Thoth who got fired from Hell's IRS for taking bribes. We gamble together with a few friends two or three nights a week. He has a Bast for a steady lady who works Shanty Town. She passes on a lot of gossip. She heard about the assault at the kibbutz, shared it with him, and he told me."

Mili knew about Bast demons with their voluptuous bodies and feline heads. They'd been a real turn-on for the ancient Egyptians who had worshipped them as goddesses. Apparently, they still had what it took and were willing to put it out for the right kind of money. Talk about a cat house.

"Anyway, all the ladies could talk about today was the incident on the kibbutz. They're stunned, repulsed, and afraid. Shocked that anything like that could happen to a little girl. The whole demon network is gossiping about it."

"And why did this demon call you?" Mili asked again.

"Because he thought *you* would be the one person who could get to the bottom of what really happened. The accused was captured in Shanty Town and handed over to a mob of angry farmers from the kibbutz. They haven't strung him up, but they're going to insist on it once Lucifer learns about what happened."

"Has the victim identified him?"

"Yes, and he has a freshly bandaged puncture wound in his chest."

"So why do I need to be involved? There's nothing I could do or would do for such a man."

"The farmers holding him would agree, but the accused asked specifically for you to be involved."

Mili frowned.

"And?"

Pfot coughed as though he were hesitant to finish. But he did.

"The accused is not a man. It's a demon."

Whoa, that's a twist, Mili thought. But she still had no desire to help. A sexual predator was scum, human or demon. The lowest semen-toting form of life.

"He says he is innocent. That he was set up by a human male who stabbed him and fled."

Holy Mary, Mother of God, Mili thought. She pulled out the chair from Mardie's bedroom writing desk and sat down.

CHAPTER NINE

I'm going with you," Little Mardie declared, and put her tea cup and saucer in the sink.

"No, you are not," Mili told her.

Little Mardie spun around and looked at her mother.

"You're taking Auntie, and you're not taking me?" Her eyes were wide with hurt and upset.

Mili shook her head. She picked up her own teacup and put it in the sink.

"This is not a lark," she stated firmly. "It is an investigation of a sexual assault, a terrifying crime that has never occurred in Hell before and I don't want you anywhere near where it happened."

Mardie's eyes flared, her temper getting the better of her. Tiny flames sprouted on her shoulders.

"Don't you dare," her mother ordered, grimacing at the thought that her daughter would even think about having a tantrum. Little Mardie's flames shrank and disappeared. "Thank you," Mili acknowledged. "Now I have to go."

"I really don't mind staying and keeping Little Mardie company."

It was Mili's twin sister Mardie. She had been sitting silently at the table watching Mili's and Little Mardie's stand-off.

"I need you, Mardie," her twin said earnestly. She knew that rape, and rape-related topics, hit awfully close to home for her sister who had been sexually abused by their father. But she really wanted her company. "I need you to listen to what is said and help me understand."

Mili looked at her and waited.

Mardie didn't speak.

"Please, sis," Mili said, her tone needy. That surprised Mardie. Scotland Yard's hotshot fem asking for help? "We can drop Little Mardie off at the bowling alley."

Little Mardie rolled her eyes.

"Don't do the rolling your eyes thing around your father," Mili chided her. "Especially in regards to anything that has to do with bowling."

Little Mardie rolled her eyes again for her mother's benefit.

"Bowling is so juvenile," she whined. "Rolling a ball down a wooden straightaway and knocking over pins. Yikes. Don't sign me up."

"At least it's not a bunch of dumb lugs tackling each other like American football."

"No," Little Mardie agreed. "The dumb lugs bowling at Avalon Lanes stab each other with knives."

"I heard *that* was actually done by a fan."

"And what does that tell you?" Little Mardie asked.

"Might be a good idea for you not to roll your eyes around those particular folks, either," Mili told her.

Her sister laughed out loud, and even Little Mardie giggled, finding her mother's advice funny in a way that only a nascent teenager could.

Mardie took her tea cup and saucer to the sink.

"Tally ho," she announced. "The game is afoot."

Mili stared at her, irritated.

"The *game*, as you call it, is an allegation of attempted rape. And if you must use a Conan Doyle cliché, at least get it right. The game, in this case, is not afoot, it's a tadger."

Both Mardie and Little Mardie stood still and stared at Mili. It was a good thing that tweeting had never been launched in Hell. If it had, there'd be a lot of tadger retweets flooding cyberspace.

* * *

"Pfot, I hate that car," were Mili's first words coming down the front steps and seeing that he had brought the black BMW.

Pfotenhauer sighed apologetically.

"I know Mrs. Mili, but the master drove the Volvo to the bowling alley this morning. All the chip sets have been replaced in the Bimmer though, and I can vouch for its trouble-free performance."

Mili arched an eyebrow, pursed her lips, and stared at Pfotenhauer.

"You like this car," she accused him.

Pfot blushed.

"I won't say that I don't ma'am. But I would never bring it to drive you around if I had any other option."

"Tell my husband that I demand a new car for my use. Maybe one of those electronic Teslas."

Pfotenhauer look visibly discomforted.

"They have problems, ma'am."

Mili frowned.

"Such as?"

"I've heard that they tend to catch on fire."

Mili squinted at Pfot.

"You're making that up."

"I am not!" the chauffeur said offended. "I've been told that under certain circumstances they combust and burn right down to the ground."

Mili stared at Pfotenhauer.

"That wouldn't have been my husband who told you that, would it?" she asked suddenly suspicious.

"No, Mrs. Mili," Pfot answered. "All I've ever heard the master say is that he had stock in the Prius."

Mili shook her head. She had always suspected that the skinny, uppity hybrid was too ugly to have been so successful without a bit of devilish intervention. Apparently, she was right. She got in the backseat of the BMW, and Little Mardie slid in next to her. Mili's sister took shotgun in front with Pfot. He got in the driver's seat and turned on the car.

In moments the air conditioning was on full and the car felt like Heaven on ice. As Pfot pulled away from the house, Mili made a mental note to ask Lucifer to assign some security demons to guard their home. Dingus and Dongus, the two Shapeshifter devils who watched the gate at the property entrance, would not be coming anywhere near the house. With a little bit of luck though, they might intercept anyone intent on deflowering her daughter and use their smuggled Korean machine guns to blow the perp to smithereens.

Deflowering? Mili reflected. What an archaic and bizarre image for losing one's virginity. And *losing* was another interesting word choice. Two equally idiotic malapropos entrenched in English vocabulary. That kind of bullshit was a thing of the past now. In these advanced times women were no longer regarded as property. They were seen as sex objects.

Mili sat quietly pondering the startling case that had been handed to her. Her twin Mardie was considering buying a Prius now that she knew who one of the investors was. Little Mardie was over her fussing and thought about the fact that Avalon Lanes had a portal she could use to venture out to San Francisco. Then she thought of the girl who someone had tried to rape down here. Maybe going to a big city by herself was best left for another day. Pfot dropped her off at the bowling

THE WICKETT SISTERS IN LIMBO

alley after kisses and hugs from Mili and Mardie. Then he headed for Shanty Town.

The roads were almost impassable out of New Babylon. Not because of traffic, but because of gaping cracks in the tarmac, deadly holes, and sections where the road had literally broken in two. Other stretches on the crumbling roadway had been removed and were now only dirt and gravel. Mili and Mardie had to hold on to keep from being thrown against the doors or the ceiling of the BMW.

Mili had only been on one worse road in her life when on loan from Scotland Yard to the president of Uzbekistan. The roads were so bad they could hardly be traversed. The one-hour trip from Bukara to Samarqand took six hours. The president told her that the blatant disrepair was to keep Soviet tanks out. She was pretty sure that the dilapidated roads were left that way to keep the citizens in.

Shanty Town was not a town. It was a contagion of one-room, hand-built shacks with brick walls and tin roofs that sprawled up the hills beyond New Babylon. To the eye, it formed an unbroken sea of suburban squalor. Makeshift electric lines purloined power from city electric, and except for the pitiful road that Pfot was driving, there were no highways through the maze.

After two hours the slums began to subside. Much to the surprise of both Wickett sisters, sagebrush began to appear alongside the road, replacing the last of the makeshift barrios. The road was still unpaved, but it was level and free of holes.

Someone was doing some work here, Mili decided, and before long the sagebrush gave way to full-grown hardwood trees like aspen, beech, and hickory. They were mature specimens with large thick trunks and gorgeous full canopies of green leaves—a whole forest of them—unlike anywhere else in Hell. In fact, Mili thought warily, this was not like Hell at all.

"Pfot," she called out. "Have you been here before?"

"No, ma'am. But I'd heard that beyond Shanty Town the land has been transformed by the folks in the kibbutz. For decades they've planted trees and put in irrigation to keep them healthy. The woods were primarily developed, however, to obscure and protect the privacy of the kibbutz."

"The people who live there must be extraordinary."

"Yes, but they're also regular folks from what I've heard," Pfot explained. "A lot more neat and tidy, however, than most of the damned down here."

"An understatement, I suspect," Mili commented.

"Well, you will soon see for yourself. The woods are giving way to the farmlands."

And indeed they did. Appearing before them for as far as they could see were cultivated fields of grain, corn, soybeans, and thick orchards bearing oranges, plums, apples, cherries, and all varieties of nuts.

Mardie shook her head.

"This is unbelievable. Do the kibbutzniks consume everything they grow?"

"Not by a long shot," Pfot said. "They trade a lot of it to buy machinery, home appliances, and air conditioners."

"From?" Mili asked.

"From demons. It's contraband, of course, but demons are paid to source what the farmers want and those that do eat pretty well to boot."

"No shit, Sherlock," Mardie commented. "Don't tell me they can smuggle in meat."

"You don't want me to tell you?" Pfot asked confused.

"Tell me," Mardie corrected herself, "I just don't want to hear it."

"They don't smuggle in meat," Pfot told her.

"Well, thank God for that."

"They smuggle in live cattle, chickens, and dairy cows."

"So these farmers can mostly do whatever they want. Does Lucifer know about all this?"

Pfot shrugged his shoulders.

"I can't say. If he does, he's never mentioned it to me."

Mili was troubled. She had grown used to the fact that Hell's demon population pretty much had free reign to run their vast black market, contracting services to Hell's residents to fetch whatever they could afford to have smuggled from Earth. Lucifer tolerated it, and in fact, benefitted from it, making sure that his own family and closest colleagues had the staples they needed and the luxuries they desired.

However, the mysterious farmers Pfot described had made things better through their own industriousness, only dealing with demon smugglers to procure what they could not produce themselves. Pfot called them kibbutzniks. Jews. But who were they, turning this corner of Hell into Paradise?

Pfot pulled off the main highway and stopped in front of a locked chain-link gate. Two men were standing behind it. One of them spoke to him through the fence. He was a short, slim man, with a shaved head. Both men were wearing jeans, boots, and long-sleeved work shirts.

"Hello," he said.

"Hello," Pfot responded. "I am Lord Lucifer's chauffeur and at the request of your establishment I have brought Milicent Morningstar, the Devil's spouse, and her sister, Mardie Wickett, to investigate a reported sexual assault on these premises."

"Thank you for coming," the man responded. "I am Aaron, and this is Jonathan. Please enter and continue on this road until you see the main complex of the kibbutz. I will call ahead and let the folks there know that you're on the way. Thank you again. Nothing like this has ever happened before. Everyone is terribly upset."

Pfot nodded, and Aaron pulled the gate open. Pfot followed a narrow paved road to a clearing where rows of buildings stood together looking like military dormitories, all of them painted white with green tile roofs. Several men were standing in front of one of the buildings, all wearing dark slacks and white short-sleeve shirts.

"Do you know any of those people?" Mili asked Pfotenhauer.

"Yes, ma'am," Pfot responded. "The gentleman who contacted me is the one with the frizzy white ring of hair around his bald head. His name is David Ben-Gurion."

Mili remembered him. The first prime minister of the newly declared state of Israel in 1948 was short and stocky with a serious expression on his lined face.

"Holy shit," Mardie exclaimed. "See the fellow next to him?"

"The one with the eyepatch?" Mili asked.

"Yes. I know him. He's Moshe Dayan. A war hero, a politician, and a one-eyed dynamo in the sack."

"You know him *that* well?"

"He was in London in the seventies. Why he was there, and what he *did* while he was there, are two different stories."

"I gather that."

Mardie grinned.

"He's a hoot, Mili. You're going to love him."

Mili stared at the men waiting. David Ben-Gurion and Moshe Dayan. She may not be with Scotland Yard anymore, but she felt the old familiar thrill of starting the hunt for a criminal who no doubt believed that he was beyond the reach of the law. She opened her car door and stepped out. She wouldn't trade Hell for anywhere else in the Universe.

CHAPTER TEN

Mili shook hands with David Ben-Gurion.

"Milicent Morningstar," she said, introducing herself. "I have to say that you are one of my great heroes."

Ben-Gurion shook her hand and blushed.

"And may I say," he responded, "that it is a pleasure to meet one of Scotland Yard's most accomplished officers *and* the wife of the Lord of Hell." The white-haired legend bowed his head in respect.

"Thank you, Mr. Ben-Gurion."

Mili turned to Moshe Dayan only to find that Mardie was already shaking his hand. The tall handsome man had a soldier's bearing, receding dark hair, and a muscular build. He didn't seem to mind that Mardie was reluctant to let go of his hand. She turned her head toward Mili.

"Moshe, this my sister Mili. Mili, this is Moshe Dayan, Israel's greatest general."

"And Israel's greatest ladies' man," Ben-Gurion added.

Moshe grinned without any hint of embarrassment.

"You're just jealous," he responded.

"Damn straight, I am. Maybe I should have had an eyepatch like yours."

"Wouldn't hurt, I have to tell you." Moshe looked at Mili. "I was spying with the British during the Mandate and some son of a bitch sniper makes the shot of a lifetime and shoots my eye out right through my binocular lens. I was just happy to still be alive until I realized that my days as a beau were over. Yet oddly enough, my opportunities increased tenfold after I got this patch."

"Didn't hurt that you're a gorgeous hunk," Mardie almost purred.

Moshe laughed. Then he gazed at her carefully.

"I know you, don't I?"

Mardie nodded.

"Seventies in London," she replied. "I never forgot."

"You still look fetching all these years later," Moshe complimented her. "How did you wind up down here?"

"Wrong choices my whole life," Mardie replied, not really answering his question. "And you?"

"Mostly for adultery, I would guess."

"Good a reason as any," Mardie said.

"And better than most," Ben-Gurion chipped in. "In my case, I neglected the obligation to do unto others as I wanted them to do unto me."

"The Golden Rule?"

"Yes."

"So you wound up in Hell?"

Ben-Gurion spread his arms wide.

"Looks that way to me," he said and chuckled.

"But what about the courageous heart you bore for Israel and the sheer grit it took to fight year after year for a Jewish homeland?"

"Earned me a nation for Jews, but truth be told, the Arabs in and around our new nation meant nothing to me. I'd have driven each and every one of them into the sea if I could have."

"Sort of the Silver Rule, eh?" Mardie asked. "Do unto others as fast as you can."

Ben-Gurion chuckled again.

"Yes. And I still feel the same way."

"Might as well," Mardie approved. "You're already fucked."

Both Ben-Gurion and Dayan laughed loudly.

Mili stepped in.

"You are aware that just because they're not here, many Muslim Arabs have been damned to Musselman Hell for deeds against Israel."

"I do know that," Moshe spoke up. "Put a parcel of them there myself."

Everyone fell silent. The atmosphere of the visit suddenly darkened and there was discomfort at where the conversation had gone. Mili took the opportunity to introduce the topic of why she and Mardie had come.

"May I hear what is known about the alleged assault?" she asked. "All I have are the scant details conveyed to our driver and aide, Mr. Paul Pfotenhauer."

Both Israelis nodded toward Pfot.

"*I* made the call," Ben-Gurion said, "at the request of the accused. Ordinarily I would have simply appealed to Lucifer's justice, but the apparent perpetrator not only swore that he was innocent, he insisted that *you* be contacted, vociferously declaring all the while that you alone would be able to prove that he had been unjustly accused."

"That remains to be seen," Mili replied. "The fact is, however, I'm here now. And I am willing to hear from each of the parties involved. I want to see the young girl who claims to have been assaulted and the prisoner who proclaims that he is not guilty despite being ID'd by the stab wound in his chest."

"He's guilty as hell," Mardie announced.

Mili stared at her.

"We don't know that yet, do we?"

"Sure we do. We just can't *prove* it yet."

Mili turned to Ben-Gurion.

"Is there a place where I can meet with each principle, one after the other?"

"Certainly. We have a small library that is near."

Mardie put her arm through Moshe's.

"Moshe is going to show me around the kibbutz while you do your interviews," said, gazing at Dayan's somewhat embarrassed face. "Right?"

"It would be my pleasure," Moshe told her. "But I have to warn you, it's mostly produce and animals. I'm not sure how interesting that will be."

"On *your* arm it will be charming." Mardie gave Moshe her hundred-watt smile.

"Then so shall it be," he replied.

"Just come back," Ben-Gurion added and winked at Mardie. Then he addressed Mili again. "How long will you need for your interviews, Mrs. Morningstar?"

"An hour total. Plus or minus."

"There's your window, Moshe," Ben-Gurion told Dayan. "Don't be tardy."

Moshe nodded and escorted Mardie away from the kibbutz buildings, back up the road, and toward the orchards. Ben-Gurion and Mili walked up the steps to the concrete block structure that served as the community's library. Mili looked back over her shoulder at Mardie. Her sister was looking back at her as well. Mili pointed at her watch. Mardie waved, happily acknowledging that she had Moshe Dayan to herself for a whole hour.

✳ ✳ ✳

Moshe held Mardie's hand and entered the orchards occupying innumerable acres of land just beyond the kibbutz buildings.

"What do you grow here?" Mardie asked.

"Everything citrus," Moshe replied. "And beyond these orchards are thousands of acres of truck gardens producing lettuce, tomatoes, onions, cabbage, cucumbers, squash, and so on and so forth. Some of the produce we sell to middlemen. Some we barter to demon consortiums in exchange for farm equipment and tools. The rest we consume on the kibbutz."

"How many people live here?"

"About ten thousand."

"That must be all the Jews in Hell."

Moshe smiled.

"Not likely. The Jews who choose to live here want a healthy and social lifestyle. Some are quite religious. Many other Jews down here prefer to live in New Babylon for the express purpose of making money. They live in fine homes with all the amenities that money can provide."

"Just like Earth," Mardie commented.

"Just like Earth," Moshe agreed.

"So why are you living on the kibbutz?" Mardie asked. "Are you religious?"

Dayan's eyes went wide with surprise.

"I'm not religious. I don't even believe in God."

"What?" It was Mardie's turn to be surprised.

"I believe in Lucifer. I've seen him. I've never seen God."

"But you're one of his chosen people."

"Says who? The feisty little bastards with chips on their shoulders who wrote the Scriptures?

Or the invading Hebrews who occupied the little strip of land called Israel only to have their asses handed to them by every neighbor that wanted access to the Mediterranean? Five thousand years of conquest, slavery, taxation, destruction, wandering, and genocide. If that's chosen, then un-choose me, please."

"Do other people on the kibbutz feel like you?"

"Almost every one of them. Although we have some religious folk, the kibbutz is not a religious community. It is however, a Jewish community. We're all kosher. All the men are circumcised. All the women are mothers. And we honor the great heroes and traditions of our people."

"But hardly anyone believes in God?"

"We mostly prefer to believe in ourselves. Much safer."

Mardie chortled.

"So you're not really here because of adultery, are you?"

"No," Moshe replied. "That's not likely a damnable sin, no matter how much rabbis and preachers huff and puff. I am down here—and I should tell you that I grew up on a kibbutz and am truly happy to be living on one again—because I led Israeli army commando raids on Arab terrorists, the Fedayeen, back in 1956."

"And?"

"And a lot of the men and boys who were shot may not have been terrorists."

"You killed innocent people?"

"There were no innocents among the Arabs," Moshe replied sternly. "Fathers, sons, wives, and daughters all equipped and blessed the terrorists. They were guilty of murder against Israeli settlers in the Sinai, and every one of them deserved to die whether they were holding a weapon or not."

Mardie let go of Moshe's hand.

"What?" he asked indignantly.

"You have blood on your hands."

Moshe shrugged disrespectfully.

"And you don't?" he snapped. "I don't suppose you have been condemned to Hell for adultery either."

Mardie flushed. And apologized.

"I'm sorry. I have no right to judge you," she replied.

"Not going to cast the first stone after all?" Moshe asked.

"Jesus Christ, you are not," Mardie teased.

"No, I'm not," Moshe agreed. "And I've had a lot of sex because of it."

"Your eyepatch *is* kind of a turn-on," Mardie said softly.

"I think I am remembering you now," Moshe mused. "Weren't you the girl who took my eyepatch off in bed and tried it on?"

"Yes, I did."

"And didn't you look inside my eye socket and pass out?"

"Only to wake up and find you inside *my* socket."

Moshe grinned and wagged his head in wonder.

"That was you."

* * *

Ben-Gurion led Mili into the small kibbutz library. Four bookcases lined one wall and there were several wooden tables and chairs. Didn't seem like all that many volumes. But most people didn't read on Earth *or* in Hell, so it was unlikely these few hundred books would get read all that quickly. There were windows in the walls left and right and natural light filled the room. Homey. Nice. Empty.

"Where is everyone?" she asked Ben-Gurion. She took a moment to study his chubby, exuberant face. Lots of energy for a man in his late eighties. Heavy, but not fat. Straight posture. Bald. Fringe of white hair spun up like cotton candy above both ears.

"Everyone has chores during daylight hours," David responded. "Only at night do folks come here to read or visit a bit. There are other places to socialize, but the non-drinkers, non-smokers, and scholars come here."

"Do you?"

"No," Ben-Gurion answered. "I have a nice little library in my private quarters."

"What do you read?"

"German classics. Modern Hebrew novels. And a few special books I have the black-market traffickers bring down for me."

"Such as?"

"Kurt Vonnegut. Isaac Asimov. Hannah Arndt. Oh, and Amos Oz—don't tell anyone."

Mili smiled.

"What can you tell me about the girl I am about to meet?"

"Not a lot." Ben-Gurion furrowed his brow. "She's been in Hell for a very long time, living in New Babylon. She asked to join the kibbutz the moment word went around that such a settlement was being considered. That was decades ago."

"What is the girl's name?"

"Brigitte. She's French. Speaks English though."

"How does she get along here?"

"Very well. Her main responsibilities are harvesting fruit and nuts, and she is a great cook in the communal kitchen. The demon who attacked her did so when she was in the orchards selecting oranges ripe for picking."

"When she reported the incident, how did she act?"

"Furious. She trembled when she told me what happened, hatred in her voice."

"How about her appearance? Disheveled, bruised, hurt?"

"None of those things. She stabbed the attacker and escaped before he could do much more than express his desires."

"He flirted?"

"He tried to pull her pants off."

"Not the same thing."

"He grabbed her from behind and threw her to the ground."

"Had she ever seen a demon before?"

"Yes. Devils are everywhere. Both on official business and talking to everybody about bringing things down here from Earth."

"All right. Thank you, Mr. Ben-Gurion. Can you bring Brigitte in now?"

"Of course. She's in the orchard, so it will take a few minutes for me to have her fetched."

"I'll peruse your library shelves."

"The books are in Hebrew."

"Oh. Of course," Mili replied feeling like a dolt. "I'll just wait, thank you."

* * *

Mardie and Moshe wandered into the citrus groves searching for oranges that had fallen to the ground. The air was fragrant and Mardie felt almost giddy breathing the heady perfume.

Moshe picked up a perfect orange and held it out to her.

"You eat it," she told him. "I'll find one on my own."

Mardie wandered on, enchanted with the luxurious citrus grove. She'd never been in a place like this on Earth. Didn't even know where one could be found unless it was California or Florida. It was especially amazing to experience this in the very midst of Hell. An oasis of goodness in the heart of a perpetual wasteland.

She looked back. Moshe had plopped down on the ground and was peeling his orange. She turned back toward the endless orchards and kept walking. She strolled on and on, heedless of anything except the paradise surrounding her. And then she sighted a man in the distance watching her. He stared at her for an endless moment, then ducked behind a tree. Mardie knew who it was. She opened her mouth and screamed.

CHAPTER ELEVEN

Mili sat at one of the tables in the library and waited for Brigitte. She gazed at the bookcases against the far wall. She knew very little about Jewish literature, even its Magnum Opus, the Hebrew Bible. She had taken a course at Oxford called the Formation of the Torah and had been surprised to learn that the earliest surviving written texts were not all that old, with at least four major literary traditions grafted together to produce the appearance of a homogeneous Scripture.

Sort of a Wikipedia for prophets, priests, kings, scribes, censors, critics, emendators, propagandists, condensers, stylists, and commentators. Did such a long engineering process worked by so many hands dilute the claim that the Hebrew Bible was divine? Who cared? Only a smattering of Ultra-Orthodox Jews and Christians even read it anymore, and they lived in the past. Everyone else looked forward. Even the Jews here in Hell.

Ben-Gurion said that the settlers were healthy, self-sufficient, and as bold as they had been on Earth. Mili was sure that David and such folk were just plain good no matter what God in his wisdom had decreed about their eternities. So good, in fact, that their reforestation, vegetable farming, and cultivated orchards were not only producing whole and perfect food, but also such vast quantities of pure oxygen that even Hell itself was being affected, even forcing the perpetually gray skies to retreat.

Satan didn't know it yet, but this kibbutz was the source of all the upheaval occurring in his kingdom, changing the very nature of Hell. He had clearly observed it, but no one had stepped forward to explain it to him. Not the kibbutzniks. Not the black market demons. And not Mili.

The library door opened. In walked a girl. She was skinny, with long, greasy brown hair and a face that might have looked like a young Catherine Deneuve if all its prettiness hadn't been stamped out by anger and resentment. She wore a white tank top without a bra and jeans. Ben-Gurion waved at Mili from the doorway, but did not enter. He left the door open and waited outside.

Mili stood up.

"Hello. My name is Mili."

"Brigitte," the girl responded.

Mili extended her hand toward the chairs around the table.

"Sit where you like."

Mili sat down.

Brigitte sat in a chair across the table from her. She studied Mili's face for a few moments, then spoke.

"Thanks for coming. To be honest, I didn't think anyone would believe me. I've been in Hell for hundreds of years and this is the first time that someone has listened."

"Has it been unsafe down here for you?"

Brigitte nodded vigorously.

"I'm probably the youngest piece of ass anywhere around and I've had to deal with lots of jerks."

"Is that why you carry a knife?"

"Actually, it's a work blade. I never needed it for anything else before I was attacked. I always felt safe and believed that the men in the kibbutz were gentlemen. I still think they are. The creature that jumped my bones was a demon from Hell."

"Where did you live before the kibbutz?" Mili asked.

"I was on my own," Brigitte answered. "Living in one dump or another. Always having to defend myself from morons who thought I needed to get laid. And my parents are down here. I've lived with them more than once, but I can't stand their endless kvetching about the French nobility. Who gives a flying fuck anymore?"

"How did you find this place?"

"Demons."

"Why would they tell you?"

"They thought I needed a place where I would be safe. I had to turn a hundred tricks for their patrons to get directions here."

"Demons pimped for you?"

Brigitte looked disgusted.

"They pimped for themselves, lady."

"Quite right. Sorry."

"It's done and I'm here. I work hard. I have friends. And I feel safe. Or I did."

"Tell me what happened."

"I work in the orange groves. A lot of the younger women do. There's a lot of walking and a lot of picking and hauling as the fruit ripens. Anyway, I was finishing up yesterday and it was getting dark. I was carrying a full basket of oranges when I was grabbed from behind. One hand clamped my mouth shut and the other one grabbed my hair. I dropped my basket and struggled to get free.

"I was pushed down to the ground and the attacker put his foot on my back. As he tried to rip down my pants, I pulled my knife out of my belt. I reached around and stabbed him in the calf. He cried out and fell. Then I stabbed him in the chest. He let go, and I ran for my life."

"The attacker let go?"

"The demon let go."

"And you have identified him as your attacker?"

"Yes. Men in the orchards heard me screaming and tracked the demon to Shanty Town. They brought him here. I saw the stab wound in his chest and knew it was the attacker."

"Did you recognize his face?"

"I never got a look at his face. All I could think of was getting away."

Mili remembered that the demon in question claimed that he'd been stabbed by the perp and left to take the rap. Now she had learned that Brigitte had not really seen the attacker's face. Was the devil really a patsy? The impossible had suddenly become the probable.

"How are you feeling now?" Mili asked.

"Good enough to go to work today."

"Okay. If I need you to identify the demon, or at least his wounds, are you willing to do so?"

"Gladly. Might even stab the bastard again given half a chance."

"You are a bit of a handful, Brigitte. But I guess you know that."

"I know that and embrace it, Mili."

"Thank you, Brigitte. I will get back to you."

Brigitte stood.

"Thank you for coming," she said.

"You're welcome. Thank you for being straightforward and honest."

"Not a problem."

Mili rose and escorted Brigitte to the open doorway. Ben-Gurion was sitting in an old-fashioned wooden lawn chair painted Kelly green, the likes of which had once dotted Brighton's beaches in the 1920s. He was reading a paperback book. He saw Mili and Brigitte leave the library, got up, stuck the book in the back pocket of his slacks, and walked over.

"Done?" he asked.

"For now," Mili answered. "Brigitte provided thorough if somewhat provocative information."

Brigitte grinned as though she were being complimented. Ben-Gurion looked puzzled. He told Brigitte she was free to go and that her work shift was done for the day. She walked off and in moments disappeared down the rows of kibbutz dormitories.

David looked at Mili.

"Provocative?" he repeated.

"She never got a look at the assailant's face. She made a positive ID based on the stab wound in his chest."

"And the calf as well?"

"No. She wasn't asked to inspect it. Have the demon brought to me and I'll look for myself."

Ben-Gurion pulled an iPhone out of his pants pocket.

"My," Mili said very surprised. "You have a mobile phone?"

"Everyone on the kibbutz has one. We've got repeater cells in the groves and forests."

"My," Mili said again.

"Josh," Ben-Gurion spoke into his phone. "Please bring the prisoner to the library.

Mrs. Morningstar is ready to interview him."

He punched the *Off* button and stuck his phone back in his pants.

"What did you think of Brigitte?" Ben-Gurion asked.

"She was cooperative and well-mannered," Mili commented.

David nodded.

"She had some adjustments when she first came to live on the kibbutz," he said. "Trusting us was not easy for her after being pawed by endless lowlifes."

"I think living here has helped her mature," Mili replied. "Something her parents were not capable of."

"Real savages, those two. They keep asking your husband to hand over Napoleon for a bit of slapping around."

"He wasn't part of the nobility," Mili said, puzzled at their request.

"Napolean didn't want their support and had them executed for murder."

"Well, that could rankle."

"Indeed. But I can relate. I still dislike Israel's old enemies."

"The Arabs?"

"The Romans."

"Zounds!"

Ben-Gurion's eyebrows shot up.

"Haven't heard that expression before," he said amused.

"It means God's wounds," Mili told him.

"I know what it means. I just never heard anyone use it. It was Medieval slang for Jesus' wounds. Sorry Jehovah didn't get his own little taste of those."

"For allowing the Romans to rule Israel?"

"*And* allowing the Spanish Inquisition, the pogroms of the Russian Czars, and worst of all, the Nazi's genocide."

"Zounds, indeed."

Ben-Gurion noticed that Brigitte had left her basket of fruit by the library steps.

"Like to have an orange?"

"Sure."

Mili looked at Ben-Gurion's gentle, wise visage.

"How did you know that zounds referred to Jesus' wounds?" she asked him.

"I know because I have sympathy for that man," David replied, looking through the oranges for a prize specimen. He found what he was looking for and handed the champion to Mili. Then he shook his head and added, "The ideas though that Jesus' mother put into his head!"

✳ ✳ ✳

Moshe Dayan ran to where Mardie was standing.

"What's wrong?" he asked.

"There!" Mardie cried, pointing into the orange groves. "A man was spying on me!"

92

Moshe took off at a run in the direction Mardie pointed. He checked behind every tree but couldn't find anyone. Mardie waved him back. Had she imagined the black-haired, lanky man staring at her? Had the news of the young woman being attacked in the kibbutz resurrected all her own fearful memories?

"Are you sure there was someone watching you?" Moshe asked.

"As sure as anything," Mardie answered. "Yet could I swear to it? Not for a moment."

Moshe frowned.

"Coming hard on the heels of yesterday's attack, it could well be the same person," he said.

"I thought that suspect has been apprehended," Mardie stuttered.

"A *suspect* has been apprehended, and your sister is trying to determine if the demon being blamed is indeed the perpetrator."

Mardie nodded. But her real concern was not the demon Mili would vet. Her real concern was whether or not the man in the orchard, real or imagined, was Morgan James Wickett.

✳ ✳ ✳

Ben-Gurion stood by the library entrance and thanked the man who'd brought the demon Brigitte had identified as her attacker. He was a fairly tall devil, maybe five foot seven, handcuffed, and wearing Speedo shorts and flip-flops. He had a large bandage taped to the center of his chest. He was cinnamon-colored with a pleasant face reminiscent of the American Hollywood actor Glenn Ford.

Ben-Gurion led the demon into the library. Just seeing the kindly expression on his face made Mili doubt that he was the one who had tried to rape Brigitte. She pointed to a chair. The demon sat. She did as well. Ben-Gurion closed the door and stood in front of it.

"What's your name?" Mili asked.

"Glenn. Because I look like—"

"Glenn Ford," Mili interrupted. "Got it. He was a pretty nice guy. Not like you, apparently."

"The accusations against me are untrue," the demon said calmly. "I buy oranges from the kibbutz and I was in the fields inspecting fruit. Nothing else."

"Explain, please."

"I buy oranges from here and sell them to food stores and restaurants in New Babylon."

Mili looked at David Ben-Gurion.

He nodded.

"A demon enterprise?" Mili asked.

"*My* enterprise," the demon corrected. "And it's a totally legitimate business. No dirty money. No black market connections. I'm just a middleman making a living. Yesterday I was inspecting the oranges, deciding how much to buy, when I was literally knocked off my feet into the dirt. I looked up to see who had run me down, only to have a large white man bend over and plunge a knife into my chest. I don't wear shirts and a spring of blood shot out of my naked chest.

"I covered it with my hand and put pressure on the wound while the demented son of a bitch ran like hell. Fearing for my life I ran too and hours later made it to Shanty Town. I went to a clinic to have my wound treated only to be surrounded by kibbutzniks who dragged me back here. My hands were tied and I was left alone locked in a building until Mr. Ben-Gurion brought in a young woman. She stared at me and identified me as the assailant who had attacked her in the orange groves."

"The end," Mili finished.

"No!" the demon cried, panicking. "If I get blamed for this I will be tortured and disfigured for a crime I did not commit."

Mili studied the upset devil. The demon doth protest too much, methinks.

"Stand up and walk a few feet away from the table," she ordered him.

The demon stood up and walked a dozen feet away. As he walked Mili looked at both of his bare calves. Neither one showed evidence of being stabbed. The demon turned and faced her.

"David," she said, addressing Ben-Gurion. "Brigitte claims she stabbed the male who was assaulting her in the calf. Then in the chest. However, she told me that she did not get a clear look at the attacker's face. I believe that Glenn here is innocent and may be released."

Ben-Gurion stepped forward searching his pants pocket for the key to the handcuffs. Glenn, the demon, sighed audibly, relieved at being found innocent of the heinous crime of which he had been accused.

Handcuffs unlocked, Glenn went down on one knee before Mili.

"Dear Madam, you are made of fairer stuff than anyone I ever met in Hell. Thank you."

"Thank you," Mili muttered, complimented and embarrassed.

Glenn rose, smiled, and glanced at Ben-Gurion who nodded toward the door. The demon was only too glad to scurry out to freedom.

"So," Mili said, "we are now out of suspects."

"Well, someone did the deed," David responded. "And I and everyone else on the kibbutz will work with you until you find out who it was."

"You are absolutely positive it couldn't be anyone living here?"

"Completely. And I believe that whoever it was will come back and try again. Brigitte looks young enough to be someone's adolescent daughter and the person who preyed on her has a taste for that, trust me. With no children in Hell the fiend will have no choice but to return. And this time we will be ready for him."

"To see that justice is done."

"Yes. Especially the torture and disfigurement part."

Mili stared at Ben-Gurion.

There wasn't a hint of amusement or teasing on his face. It is appointed for men once to die and after that the judgment. One of her Christian colleagues at the Yard always made that remark whenever a criminal died in prison. The only judgment down here was the threat of Satan's torture and disfigurement. *He* decided who got what. She decided to keep that in mind the next time Lucifer wanted to tie her up in bed.

CHAPTER TWELVE

Mardie walked into the library as pale as a ghost. She sat down, utterly silent, her eyes glazed over. Ben-Gurion brought a bottle of cold water from a refrigerator and urged her to drink. She took the bottle, but only drank a sip. Mili motioned Dayan to step away and led him to a corner.

"What happened?" Her voice was tense, almost as though Moshe himself was guilty of whatever had occurred.

"We were strolling through the orange groves," Moshe began, his voice almost a whisper. "Mardie saw a man watching her. When she called to me he fled, and I couldn't find him anywhere."

"Do you think it was the same man who attacked Brigitte and the demon?"

"I can't say." Moshe paused, looking straight at Mili's face. "Mardie was sure that the man was her father."

Mili stared back horrified. Then she walked over to her sister.

"Mardie?" she said.

Mardie gazed absently at Mili for a moment. Mili thought she might be in shock.

"It was him, Mili," Mardie finally said. "I have no doubt that it was him."

Mili put an arm around her shoulders.

"I believe you. I am so sorry you had to experience that."

"Every part of me is afraid, Mili. I panicked thinking he had hunted me down."

"It's more likely that he's the one who attacked Brigitte and returned to where he found her the first time."

"This man is your father?" Moshe asked.

Mili nodded.

"Neither you or your sister ever saw him down here?"

"No. I suspect he preferred it that way."

And so the conundrum. Mili would have to pursue Morgan Wickett as a likely suspect in the attack on Brigitte. Mardie had seen and identified him lurking in the orchard with her own eyes. But in doing her job, she would be drawing Mardie into a web of horror, exposing her to the man who had, in fact, attacked and raped her. She knew she had no choice but to do her duty, yet was there any way to spare Mardie?

"David?" She spoke to Ben-Gurion. "I think I have a plan."

✳ ✳ ✳

The African Dictators had drawn first position in the semifinal game against The European Dictators. Idi Amin of Uganda stood at the top of the alley ready to bowl the first ball of the contest. Joseph Mobutu of Zaire sat on the team bench, along with Jean-Bedel Bokassa of the Central African Republic, and Muammar Gaddafi, late of Libya. Before Lucifer could blow his whistle to start the competition, a shrill female voice cried from the gallery seats.

"Amin, you walrus, stand aside and let one of your betters start this game!"

Idi Amin spun around and searched the gallery for the speaker of the snide remark.

Alice Roosevelt stood up.

"Are you looking for me, you fat sack of dung?" she taunted Amin.

Idi stared at Alice in disbelief.

"I bet you can't see me with your one remaining piggy eye, can you?" she taunted.

Amin charged the gallery like a bull rampaging through Pamplona's alleys. He drove straight for Alice Roosevelt even as her father jumped up to protect his obstreperous daughter. Teddy stepped in front of her just as the stampeding king of Uganda lowered his head. He rammed the president's chest.

Watching Teddy crash backwards over the seats behind him, the two Samn referees rushed for the gallery. In the moment before the ferocious devils arrived, Alice Roosevelt took aim at Idi Amin's remaining good eye and jammed the gold tip of her parasol through it all the way into his brain.

Before she could withdraw it the Samns ripped her body to pieces and proceeded to do the same to Idi Amin, who was clutching his face and howling in agony. Unfortunately, the raging demi-gods were incapable of backing off their destructive frenzy and proceeded to rip up President Roosevelt and another dozen or so spectators before managing to stop.

Satan blew his whistle, furious at the sheer stupidity of everyone involved in the goddamn ruckus: Alice, Teddy, Idi, and the pair of out-of-control demons. A lesser lord than Lucifer would probably just have the gore mopped up and go on with the tournament. But Lucifer had pride, as misplaced as it might seem in these moronic circumstances. Plus, he just hated the fact that the gallery of *his* bowling alley now looked like a claymore mine had taken out a huge batch of fans.

He ordered the Samns to stand down and he cancelled the game.

"Please leave now," he told the folks who were staring in horror human body parts draped on the seats, collapsed on the floor, and leaking blood and guts all over everything. "The game will be rescheduled."

Lucifer didn't have to repeat himself. Everyone got up and left instantly.

Satan surveyed the mess and spoke to the Samns again.

"Separate who's who in this mess and bag them separately. Call me when you're done. Then and only then will I make an appointment with the Almighty and try to explain what happened here."

With a little bit of luck, God would refuse new Hellion bodies for Idi and Alice. Satan shook his head and smiled at the happy thought. More likely though, Jehovah would insist that everyone be recreated. Hell was, after all, intended to be eternal for every victim, and that included Idi Amin and Miss Alice Roosevelt.

✳ ✳ ✳

Mili and Mardi had returned from the kibbutz and were drinking Irish coffees in Mardie's kitchen. Mardie loved her little kitchen, anchored by her black-enamel cast iron Andre Godin stove. As awesome as that French stove was, however, the room's true masterpiece was the marquetry-topped kitchen table.

The kitchen had maple cupboards, Dutch blue-and-white tile counter backsplashes, and lace curtains with embroidered daisies and tulips on her one narrow window. Last—but dearly beloved in terms of loyal service—was her McCray wooden ice box, an antique altogether more reliable than any other refrigerating unit in Hell.

Mardie took great comfort being safe in her own home. The attack at the kibbutz and then seeing her father had rattled her more than anything else she had ever experienced down here. Mili understood and respected Mardie's reluctance to talk about the terrible experience. On the other hand, she wanted to help Mardie to be brave, to refuse to be intimidated, and to stand up strong and confront the man who had done her wrong. Mili poured more coffee into both of their cups, topped them off with some Jameson's, and added several spoons of sugar and more cream to hers.

"Have you got anything sweet to eat around here?" she asked.

Mardie nodded.

"There's Marionberry ice cream in the ice box."

"Marionberry? What is that?" Mili asked.

"I don't know. It came with the stuff from Heaven yesterday."

"I'd like to try some, please."

"Just the carton, no bowl?"

"The way nature intended," Mili said.

"You mean God?"

"Him, too," Mili answered.

Mardie fetched the quart of Marionberry ice cream. She took the top off the round container and stuck a teaspoon in the purple-swirled ice cream. She set it down in front of Mili.

"I love you," Mili told her.

"You're easy. What if it had been just plain vanilla?"

"Then I'd like you."

"Ha!" Mardie snorted.

She watched Mili dig into the ice cream like a dwarf mining the depths of Lonely Mountain. Diabetes-free and sporting her beautiful new Hellion body, ice cream could do Mili no harm. Unlike their father who had now appeared on her horizon. Mardie frowned at the thought.

Mili saw it.

"Are you thinking about what happened today?"

Mardie looked up.

"Is it that obvious?"

"Afraid so."

"I always knew he was down here. Had to be. But seeing him after all these years was a shock."

"Did Moshe fill you in on the details about the attack on the kibbutz woman?"

"He did," Mardie answered. "Everybody seemed pretty sure that a demon had gotten out of line."

"Nope," Mili countered. "The demon was a patsy, stabbed by the real perp to play the red herring. Whoever tried to rape Brigitte set him up and escaped."

"And then Morgan Wickett shows up."

"An odd and disturbing coincidence," Mili agreed.

"No such thing as a coincidence, sis," Mardie observed. "The old bastard has a taste for girls. Let's just say it. Brigitte is young, pretty, and vulnerable. Or so Morgan thinks. I wonder if he stalked her prior to attacking her."

"If he did, he managed to miss the fact that she carried a knife in her belt."

"He deserved what he got," Mardie told her.

"You won't get an argument from me."

Mardie shook her head and drank down her Irish coffee. Mili watched her for a moment and then broached the one subject she really didn't want to raise.

"I have to track him down, Mardie. I'd like your support."

"I hate him."

"This is Hell. That's okay."

Mardie stared at Mili, then laughed.

"I *love* it down here," Mardie said. "Most folks are more upright and pleasant than people on Earth. And we have discovered a little kibbutz that has carved out a bit of paradise. Blue skies. Pure water. Flowers and trees. I love it down here."

Mili reached across the table and patted Mardie's hand.

"I love it down here, too, and I've been thinking about how to make my own wee contribution to everyone's happiness. I've bribed two demons at the bank to help me and I've applied for a loan through a third demon. I want to set up Ben and Jerry's ice cream stores all over Hell."

Mardie stared at her sister. Ben and Jerry's? Down here?

"All right, speak up," Mili said watching her. "What are you thinking?"

"I'm wondering who will get Little Mardie when Lucifer divorces you."

"Get serious. Think how much misery could be diminished by a simple ice cream cone once in a while."

"Neither God nor Lucifer will approve such a thing. It flies in the face of the inconvenience and unhappiness that is Hell's charter."

"Right, unless you have money or connections. *Then* it's okay to have some happiness."

"There is that," Mili agreed.

"When do you propose to tell your husband?" Mardie asked.

"I don't propose to tell my husband."

Mardie arched an eyebrow in disbelief.

"No?"

"No. I can set up a blind corporation and run the Ben and Jerry's outlets myself. No one will be able to dig down far enough to find my involvement."

"Don't fool yourself into thinking that. Lucifer will find out," Mardie said worried.

"Then I'll deal with him when and if it happens," was Mili's retort.

"Don't say I didn't warn you," Mardie said. She saw that her twin had finished the carton of ice cream.

"Did you like the Marionberry?" she asked.

"Quite. Wish there was more."

"There is."

"Goodness sake!" Mili exclaimed. "May I?"

"Yes. You might as well have one last happy binge before Lucifer rakes you over the coals."

Mili frowned with apprehension.

"You don't suppose he'll use real coals, do you?"

"Count on it," Mardie answered. "And you won't be eating any ice cream after that for a long, long time."

✳ ✳ ✳

Avalon Lanes had been cleaned up. Using brooms, mops, buckets of water, and several forty-quart heavy-duty garbage bags, the two Samn demons that had gone postal had bagged up the body parts they'd strewn all over the bowling alley. They swept and swabbed up guts, gore, blood, and miscellaneous people fluids. Cleaned every square inch again with Ajax and sponges. Then they sent the bags to be disposed of at a city dump.

At Lucifer's audience with the Almighty he petitioned to have Hellion bodies recreated for Theodore and Alice Roosevelt, Idi Amin, and those innocent bystanders who'd been swept up into odd piles of body parts and human slush. God granted his request, telling Satan in a haughty tone that he smelled of human decay, and ordered him to leave posthaste. Jehovah actually said posthaste. On his more annoying days he talked very much like the King James Bible, the stiff, uppity, condescending English translation of the Scriptures dedicated to a Divinity to match. Good grief.

Lucifer was sitting at the bar drinking Guinness Stout with Omer, one of the senior Balaam officers from Hell's Central Bank. Tall and elegant, the Balaam sat on a barstool next to him. The banker was wearing khaki-colored slacks, a green Polo shirt which complimented his red skin, and brown Dockers. Perfect business casual for meeting the boss in his bowling alley. Lucifer had on black slacks, Mazlan crocodile slip-ons, and a Turnbull & Asser dress shirt with the white collar unbuttoned. He was drinking heavily whereas the Balaam had not touched his schooner of beer.

"Pardon my foul mood, Omer," Satan told the bank official. "Two Samns had a meltdown here today that forced me to cancel an important bowling match. It's irritating and maddening. Fact is, though, I appreciate your coming all the way here. What's your concern?"

"Thank you, Lord," the banker replied. "Early this afternoon I was approached by a Mammon with whom I have done business before. He is a good customer and concentrates on start-up opportunities.

He borrows large sums and repays them on time. Today he proposed borrowing a substantial amount of money on behalf of an investment consortium wishing to start a franchise business in Hell."

"Another franchise?" Satan groaned. Hell had a lot of franchises already. Fast food, laundries, car repair, even the Hells Bells grocery stores were a franchise system.

"They want to open a chain of specialty shops."

"No guns, no knives, no bombs," Lucifer told him. "No slaves, no servants, no indentureds. No sports franchises, no themed merchandise shops, and no betting."

"Of course, sir. I know and obey the rules."

"Then you're an unusual demon," Satan said.

Omer bowed his head in acknowledgement of the Devil's compliment.

"What kind of loans has this Mammon taken out previously?" Satan asked.

"Sex toys, porn videos, brothels."

"And what does he want to promote this time?"

"Ice cream."

Satan arched an eyebrow. Yet he could see where ice cream would fit on that list.

"What are the proposed terms?"

"Three and a half million dollars. Seven-year loan. Fifty percent interest."

"Make it one hundred percent interest. Half for the bank and half for me."

"Done, sir. I take it you like ice cream?"

"No. But I love someone who does."

CHAPTER THIRTEEN

Mili got a call from Little Mardie. Her daughter complained that she was hungry and wanted to come home.

"What did you do after I dropped you off at Avalon Lanes this morning?"

"I left."

Mili waited for more.

"And?" she finally asked.

"There was a fight at the bowling alley. I walked downtown and went into a sex shop."

Mili frowned.

"Find anything interesting?" she asked, steeling herself.

"*Everything* was interesting," Little Mardie answered. "Have you ever been inside one of those places?"

"Nice girls don't go into those kinds of stores."

"I'll bet Alice Roosevelt does."

"That just proves my point."

"I didn't buy anything. Just looked."

"We'll talk more about this when your father is home."

"Please tell Pfot that I'm at the Apple store on Steve Jobs Boulevard,"

Little Mardie told her. "The staff is helping me jailbreak my iPhone."

"What's that? It sounds illegal."

"Are you pulling my shoe, Mother? There's no such thing as illegal down here. I wanted to run some third-party apps on my phone that the iPhone internals won't support. Few minutes at the Apple store and I can use whatever app I want."

"It's not really an Apple store, is it?"

"No. Does that matter?"

No, Mili thought, *it doesn't.* There were no ethics, no guidelines, no morals, and no laws in Hell. Not everything was allowable, however. Violence of every kind was banned. One could threaten and bully, but not hurt, nor murder. Anyone and everyone could have sex, but it had to be consensual. No sexual assault and no rape. The extremes had been banned, as it were, but *normal* human behaviors like lying, cheating, and adultery were acceptable. All in all, not so very different from Earthly life in London. Just safer.

"I'll send Pfot, young lady. Be there when he pulls up to the curb in ten minutes."

"Okay. Thank you."

"Any special requests for dinner?"

"How about tacos? With guacamole?"

"Can do. But we won't eat until your father can join us."

"Not sure when he's coming home, Mom," Little Mardie warned. "He had to reschedule the semifinal game because of the fight I told you about. Couple of Samn referees tore through the gallery trying to stop a fight between Alice Roosevelt and Idi Amin."

"Tore through or tore up?"

"The second one. Big time. Daddy had to go to Jehovah and arrange for a bunch of replacement bodies."

"Well, that won't have put him in a good mood."

"Nope. But he's back now and has rescheduled the game for six o'clock."

"Okay, fine. Come home and I'll cook tacos for you."

"Thanks, Mother! Loveyoumeanitbye!"

I hope so, Mili thought. Never had her daughter seemed more out of control. Little Mardie had always been brave and independent, but now she went where she wanted and did as she pleased. Usually without telling anyone. Mili had thought about restricting some of Little Mardie's freedom, but Lucifer would likely be unsympathetic. He never told Little Mardie no. Her consequent rebelliousness reminded her of what her sister Mardie had been like when they were growing up.

Mili felt a knot form in the pit of her stomach. Dear God. She'd better get birth control pills for her daughter before she found out whether or not her not-so-little Mardie could have a baby down here in Hell. She picked up her cell phone and punched in Lucifer's number. His face lit up the monitor when he answered.

"Hi, doll!" he said happily. "Got a bunch of stuff going on this second, but I never want your calls to go unanswered." He waited for Mili to speak. She could see him fidgeting.

"I heard from Little Mardie that you had to reschedule this morning's game."

"Did indeed. All's well now though."

"Is it? She told me that Alice Roosevelt and Idi Amin came to blows."

"Just Alice. She stabbed Idi in his good eye with her umbrella."

"I'm sure he had it coming."

"He did. I had Heaven leave his new Hellion blind."

"May I change subjects?"

"Of course."

"I want you to know that there is a very serious issue brewing in the countryside north of the city. A very young woman working on a farming collective was attacked, just barely fending off an attempted rape."

Lucifer scowled. Mili could hear the happy background noise of the crowd gathering in the bowling alley. The contrast between that lighthearted exuberance and Satan's grimace was depressing.

"I trust that you went out and investigated?" he asked.

"Pfot's contacts reached out through him to me," Mili answered. "I have started an investigation. I took Mardie with me out to the farm to conduct interviews and study the turf. They had a suspect who turned out not to be the perp. Much to my dismay, however, and especially Mardie's, is that she spotted our father on that collective."

"He works there?"

"No, which makes his appearance very suspicious."

"Then he's a suspect?"

"Given his past behaviors, how could he not be? Morgan James Wickett is his legal name. We know he was damned and have proof of it from the files you provided to me years ago. Will you have him located and brought in for questioning?"

"Of course."

"I know that you have a game tonight, so afterwards perhaps?"

"Yes. May I assume that you've been keeping your eye on Little Mardie during all of this?"

"Absolutely. If my father is actually guilty of this despicable attack, I would imagine that he is already well aware that the only true girl in Hell is Little Mardie. She is not safe even though she is his grand-daughter. The man is a monster who preyed upon my sister. He is now my lead suspect in this case even if I have nothing else to go on besides my suspicions."

"I wonder why he surfaced after all these years?"

"Opportunity?" Mili suggested. "Renewed interest? Maybe he is even wicked enough to set up the woman he attacked just to sidetrack us as he goes after his true target."

"Christ," Lucifer swore. "You mean Little Mardie?"

"Maybe, or maybe even *she* is no more than yet another distrac-tion, camouflaging his real target, my sister Mardie."

"Do you suspect revenge?"

"I suspect rape."

"Yes, but perhaps rape *as* revenge," Mili explained. "Hell is full of individuals harboring grudges. Demons bear grudges. Maybe even you bear a grudge."

"No," Lucifer denied. "I don't."

"Would you kill God if you could?"

"Yes."

Mili looked at her husband's face.

He stared back at her.

"And *that's* been simmering inside you for eons. My father has only been in Hell fifty years or so. A blink of eye as grudges go down here."

Mili watched small flames form on Lucifer's shoulders and race down his sleeves as he came to grips with the notion that Morgan Wickett might intend to abuse or even kill Mili's sister Mardie.

"Before the game starts tonight," he spoke through clenched jaws, "I will assign demons to keep watch over your sister and search for your father. I will be home as quickly as possible and I myself will watch over you and Little Mardie."

Lucifer gained control of his temper and the little flames died out.

"Thank you for that, darling," Mili told her husband. "Good luck with the big game. You said Idi Amin's body came back blind. Is he still going to play?"

"Blind as Oedipus he is, but he's sitting on The Potentates' team bench all the same."

"I hope he gets his arse kicked."

"Ha!" Lucifer threw his head back and enjoyed a long laugh. "Who knows? He might bowl even better blind. His other senses may compensate for the loss of vision."

"What other senses?"

"Envy, pride, lust, gluttony, greed, and wrath."

"You left out sloth."

"Yes, I did. The one thing he will not evidence is sloth."

"A speedy bowler," Mili suggested.

111

"A speedy *blind* bowler," Lucifer agreed.

"A speedy blind bowler who's going to get his arse kicked."

Satan gazed at his spouse with an amused expression.

"What's with this arse thing?"

"My small wish for a bad man to have an unpleasant game," Mili replied.

"Everyone on his team is a bad man."

"True. I hope they all get their arses kicked."

"By the evil-to-the-bone European Dictators team."

Mili was momentarily at a loss for words.

"Yes," she finally muttered. "By them. I hope they win."

"Don't share that with any Jews, Christians, Muslims, homosexuals, gypsies, preachers, teachers, intellectuals, writers, poets, priests, nuns, or professors."

"I won't."

"Bye, love."

"Bye. I'm sorry if I sounded like a narrow-minded bitch."

Satan grinned.

"I hope *all* the teams get their arses kicked," she said in farewell.

With a chortle, Lucifer ended the call.

* * *

Pfotenhauer called Mili's mobile phone.

"I am outside, ma'am, with Little Mardie. When she is safely in the house, may I speak with you for a moment?"

"Did she give you a sex toy?"

"Beg pardon?"

"Send her in and I'll come out."

Mili opened the door and Little Mardie breezed by her.

"Hug?" Mili called after her.

"Potty!" Little Mardie cried back.

Mili walked outside. Pfot was standing by the Volvo.

"What's up?" she asked him.

"Sorry to bother you," he replied quietly. "I just got a call from Moshe Dayan at the kibbutz. He's been trying to contact you. Brigitte has gone missing."

Mili narrowed her eyes and gazed at Pfotenhauer. He looked completely distraught.

"When?"

"She was working her section of the orange groves and did not return at dusk, the end of the workday. Workers had gone through the groves earlier and collected her crates of ripe oranges, but no one saw her."

"Are the fields being searched?"

"It was dark before the searches started, but the whole kibbutz is scouring the groves by torchlight."

"It will be hard to find this particular needle-in-a-haystack, but they should try to be alert to the presence of any freshly turned earth."

"A grave?"

"Precisely."

"I will call Mr. Dayan back immediately," Pfot promised. He looked at Mili. "Anything else?"

"If anyone finds the girl—or her body—she is not to be touched and I am to be called immediately."

"Absolutely."'

"Thank you, Pfot."

Pfotenhauer nodded.

"Night, Mrs. Mili."

Pfot got into the Volvo and called Moshe Dayan on his mobile.

Mili turned and went into the house. Pfot would be knocking on the door in moments if he had any more news. He did not. Mili tried not to think about the tough, little French girl who was now missing, But she did, hoping against hope that she had not been hurt by Morgan

Wickett. Stepping beyond that judgment, Mili hoped that Brigitte had not been injured by anyone. But especially not by her father.

CHAPTER FOURTEEN

It was six o'clock p.m. The appointed time to reboot the semifinal bowling match. Changed into his judge's shirt Lucifer surveyed the alley. The Potentates were gathered at their team bench. The European Dictators were at theirs. The gallery was packed. Teddy Roosevelt and his daughter Alice were sitting in the front row. Alice looked every day of her ninety-six years. Her Hellion replacement face would have to grind through endless plastic surgeries to appear as anything other than the wrinkled old hag staring at Idi Amin.

The Potentates would bowl first. Satan watched Idi Amin feel around the ball return. Whoa. If he couldn't even find his ball, how would he toss it down the alley? Being a blind politician, or a blind businessman, probably didn't matter. But being a blind bowler did. He and everyone else watching were seeing that now.

Idi found what he was looking for. Something he'd bribed one of the Samn demons to hide for him. He lifted the severed head of Alice Roosevelt's former body and held it up for her new incarnation to see. Alice scowled. Teddy passed out. And the gallery erupted in boos and hisses for Amin's tasteless prank.

Lucifer nodded at the Samn closest to Amin. The demon took the head from Idi and carried it away. The Devil got off his judge's stool and walked over to Amin.

"Idi, it's Lucifer."

The dictator frowned.

"Prove it."

"All right. Shake my hand."

Amin extended his right hand. Lucifer flamed up his own hand and shook it. Idi yanked his hand back instantly. To his credit he didn't cry out, but he did cradle his scorched right hand with his left.

"Despite your juvenile stunt with the head," Satan addressed him, "I am going to allow you to bowl with your esteemed colleagues. But I warn you, one more incident like that, you *and* The Potentates will forfeit. Understand?"

"You burned my hand!" Amin protested.

"Hopefully it will hurt your bowling."

"I don't like you."

"You're not supposed to," Lucifer replied matter-of-factly.

"Well, I don't. I wish it was your head that I had lifted and showed everyone."

The Devil smiled with amusement.

"I'll bet you do, you oleaginous piece of shite."

"You burned my hand and now you're calling me names?" Amin sneered. "What is that word you used?"

"Oleaginous," Lucifer obliged. "It means greasy."

Idi balled up his fists and raised his voice. "You think you are the big boss down here. Well, I prayed to God to help me bowl *two* Perfect Games tonight, so watch out."

That surprised Satan.

"I didn't know you were religious."

"You missed the carnage during my reign?"

"No. That's why you're here."

"I was God's humble servant."

"Shouldn't you be in Heaven then?"

"Yes, I should. Would you check into that for me?"

Lucifer shook his head. The prick had chutzpah.

"You bowl two Perfect Games tonight and I will do exactly that."

"And I want both of my eyes fixed."

"Piece of cake."

"Does that mean yes?"

"If a blind bowler can put away two Perfect Games that means yes."

Amin nodded and turned away.

Ha! Two Perfect Games. Satan was really going to enjoy watching sightless Idi Amin trying to make those happen. Ah, Hell. There was just no place like it.

✳ ✳ ✳

Mili woke up at four o'clock in the morning. Lucifer was not in bed. She could see a light coming from the living room downstairs. She got up and went to see if her husband might be there. He was. Sitting in a chair and gazing into space. He saw her and waved.

"Why aren't you in bed, sweetheart?" she asked, leaning down and giving him a peck on the cheek.

"Terrible night," he said. "Terrible night."

"At the alley?"

Lucifer nodded. His face was drawn and unhappy.

"Since we're up, why don't I fix us some coffee and you can tell me what happened," Mili suggested.

Lucifer rose and followed Mili into the kitchen. Unlike her sister, Mili evidenced little decorating taste. The kitchen had white painted cupboards with chrome pulls, white appliances, tandem white porcelain sinks, and a round green Formica table in the middle of the room with metal legs and four metal chairs padded with green cushions.

The floor was covered with pink linoleum and there was a brown-and-black hooked rug on the floor. There was no framed art, just blank walls and a white-curtained window that looked out at the woods that surrounded the house. It was home sweet home though, if you grew up poor in London in the 1950s.

Lucifer sat down at the table. Mili began to heat up the water in the Keurig coffee maker.

She turned toward her husband.

"So what is stressing you, love?"

"Stress is *exactly* what I am feeling right now," he replied. "I've been down here God knows how many millennia, yet I've never been as stressed as I am right now."

"Tell me why," Mili said.

Lucifer scowled.

"Idi Amin bowled two Perfect Games."

"And *that's* what has you so upset?"

"It's actually only the tip of the iceberg. The part below—the part no one apparently sees but me—is that something is happening down here that is not just upsetting me, it's upsetting Hell itself. I began getting the creeps when Edward threw the first Perfect Game earlier this week, and now the worst character in Hell, Idi Amin, *threw two of them in one night.*"

Lucifer looked into Mili's eyes.

"He told me before the series began that he had prayed for God to help him bowl two Perfect Games." Satan looked panicked. "And then he did!"

"That doesn't mean God helped him," Mili countered. "Although I think you're right that Hell is having issues."

"Hell *is* having issues, Mili, and whether it's God's doing or something else, the fact is things are going *north*, not south. Not only did Idi Amin toss two Perfect Games, someone applied at the bank for a loan to start a chain of ice cream shops down here. *Can you imagine?* Goes against everything we stand for."

Mili didn't respond to Lucifer's comment. Instead, she fixed his coffee, dark roast, black, and then hers, light roast, lots of milk and sugar. She brought both mugs to the table and sat down.

"I don't know what to say," she told her husband.

"Maybe you could just check around here and there over the next few days," he responded gently. "See if your detective's instincts pick up anything suspicious. My own brain tells me that nothing can change down here without God's knowledge and permission.

"But my heart reminds me that not so long ago we had a murderer dumping bodies right here on my own porch. If that could happen, then what's going on now? It's tearing me up not knowing who or what is causing these monumental changes. Christ, I'm worried sick about what might be ahead."

Mili sipped at her coffee and wondered if she should mention the kibbutz. She could not explain the profound effects the industrious kibbutz folk were having on Hell, but she had seen with her own eyes what they had done in their corner of perdition. She was convinced that the goodness they invested in the land was already seeping into the other parts of Hell.

As for the Ben and Jerry's chain, she was not going to 'fess up that the dummy corporation borrowing money was actually hers. And while she was on that subject, being charged one hundred percent interest irked her. Probably served her right though. Lucifer didn't know that Mili was the one who would be anteing up the sky-high cost. She was plotting the whole ice cream franchise thing behind his back. She'd worry about her dishonesty later. Right now, she was riding the end-justifies-the-means train.

Lucifer looked at Mili.

"Enough about my issues. What happened at the farm you visited? Any trace of your father?"

"A young female worker, a girl really, was indeed attacked and almost raped. The girl managed to stab the perp twice with her work knife. Once in the leg and once in the chest. He fled wounded and she reported the episode to the co-op management immediately. A demon was accused of the crime and apprehended. He claimed that he had been stabbed by a fleeing human. I accepted his story when I saw that he had a wound in the chest, but none in either leg."

"A demon was suspect?" Lucifer snapped. "That's impossible." The flames on his head raced down the sleeves of his judge's shirt.

"That demon was innocent," Mili said, trying to calm her husband down. "Framed by the actual perpetrator. But last night the girl who was attacked went missing in the same spot where Mardie spotted our father."

"Dear God!" Lucifer cried. "Are search parties out?"

"Yes. Ever since she didn't return from the groves."

"As soon as you have any kind of update, let me know. I can put thousands of demons into the search."

"Thank you, love." Mili squeezed his hand. "May I make you another coffee?"

"Only if you're staying up, too."

"I can't sleep, and early this morning Pfot is going to drive me and Mardie to join the search."

"Anything I can do?"

"Yes. Alert the demon network about the crime. And have pictures of Morgan Wickett uploaded to the internet with a **MAN WANTED** header."

"Consider it done. Please keep me posted on any progress."

"Thank you," Mili said, fixing their coffee refills. "By the way, who won the semifinal match tonight?"

"The Potentates," Satan moaned. "The whole team got so charged up by Amin's two Perfect Games they trounced the Europeans."

"So then it's The African Dictators competing against The British Royals for the championship?"

"Yes, a week from now. I added a few days between the matches so everyone could calm down." Lucifer gazed at Mili with a somewhat forlorn expression. "Doll, you know how precious bowling is to me, but this week the games were plagued by taunting, name calling, fist fighting, and torn up bodies. All over a goddamn game! I've already banned soccer, football, baseball, and basketball. If the final game of the tournament is as bad as the one today, I will ban bowling, too."

"No one will ever bowl again?" Mili said shocked.

"No, I'd still allow bowling," Satan clarified. "But there wouldn't be any leagues or tournament competitions."

"Wow. That would be a big change."

"Yes, and let me tell you this," Lucifer responded, tongues of fire suddenly erupting on top of his head again. "If everyone but me starts bowling Perfect Games I'm shutting down all the alleys."

"Wouldn't it be better if you just learned how to fix a game? I'd think the demons working the pin reset machines could be persuaded to help you out."

Lucifer stared at Mili in disbelief.

"Are you suggesting that I *cheat* in order to get a Perfect Game?"

"I think that's what I said. Can your demons make that happen?"

Lucifer grimaced.

"Of course they can. And it now strikes me that such mischief might already be in play. Three Perfect Games in one week? Why didn't I suspect those little bitches earlier? I'm going to have a talk this morning with the Pixies handling the pin reset machines."

"Pixies?"

"Yes. Little fallen angels who used to tend flowers in Heaven. I have them tending bowling pins now."

"And you think that Prince Edward and Idi Amin may have somehow managed to bribe them?"

"It would go a long way toward explaining why the one game that cannot be bowled down here has been bowled three times this week."

"So God may not be making things better after all?"

"At least not in my bowling alleys."

121

Mili smiled and patted Lucifer's cheek.

"I just don't know what to say," she told him.

"I do." Lucifer threw up his arms. "Praise the Lord!"

CHAPTER FIFTEEN

Pfot stopped to pick up Mardie at 7:00 a.m. and waited in front of her house twenty minutes. When Mardie came out at last she had Bowles with her, a handsome Arab man with thick, beautifully groomed salt-and-pepper hair. Since their meeting at the Good News reenactment club, they had met frequently at Mardie's house for reenactments of their own.

Bowles gave Mardie a kiss and waved cordially at Pfotenhauer. He opened a car door for her and Mardie hopped in the back of the Volvo. Pfot got back in the driver's seat, started up the car, and got on the road.

"Morning, miss," he greeted Mardie.

"Why, yes, it is," she said. "Sorry I'm late."

"No worries. I allowed for a bit of extra time between your pickup and Mrs. Mili just in case any issues arose."

"Well, *one* did," Mardie said and laughed happily. Pfotenhauer blushed. "And what about you, dear boy?" she asked. "Who do you have to help you while away the centuries we have in front of us?"

"I am not one to kiss and tell," Pfot answered shyly.

"So you've got some kissing going on?" Mardie teased. "Enough said. Good for you."

"And good for you as well, Miss. Mr. Bowles is a gem of a man."

"Yes, he is, Pfot. His mother was Moroccan and a Muslim. His father was French and a last-minute Roman Catholic. He never was religious, but when he lay dying the hospital staff called a priest who gave him last rites even though he was in a coma."

"Better late than not at all, dear lady. He might have been shipped down to Islamic Hell."

"Or maybe up to Islamic Heaven. I remember hearing that Muslims who died serving the faith were awarded a wad of virgins in Allah's Paradise."

Pfot's eyebrows shot up.

"Bloody lot of work if you ask me," he reacted.

"My, Pfot, do tell."

"Think I just did, Miss Mardie. Was that too much information?"

"Not at all. I love to hear that you know what you want, or *don't* want."

"Thanks. And I do. Though not too often at a few minutes before seven in the morning."

"Ha!" Mardie chortled. "I highly recommend it."

At that Pfot clammed up. He'd shared more about his private thoughts in the last few moments than he had ever done with anyone. It sort of overwhelmed him, but he could trust Miss Mardie to keep his confessions to herself, unlike the demons in Hell who leaked secrets at a hundred miles an hour.

Pfotenhauer pulled up in front of the gates that marked the entry to Lucifer's property. One couldn't say estate, for though the Devil and his wife owned lots of land, they lived in a simple 1940s spec home, homey and small. Its modesty sent a clear message that the ruler of Hell was a regular guy, except when he lost his temper, at which point everything around him was consumed by the Archangel of Light's firepower.

Two giraffes stood at the gate watching them approach.

"Morning, Pfot," one of them said.

"And to you—" Pfot paused.

"Steve," the Shapeshifter identified himself.

"—Steve," Pfot finished. "And hello to you, too, Butch," he greeted the other giraffe.

Steve and Butch were Lucifer's longtime demon security guards, and while Pfot found their shapeshifting abilities quite entertaining, Mili did not and intensely disliked both of them. She found them childishly adolescent at best, and low-grade morons at worst.

Steve the giraffe pressed a button with his nose that electronically opened the gates, and nodded in a stately fashion to Pfotenhauer as he drove through heading up the drive to the master's house. It was hard to believe that it had been almost twenty years since he'd brought Mardie and Hugh Everett to confront the serial killer who'd been dumping his victims' bodies on the Devil's porch.

He would have sworn then that Mili would never forgive her sister's crimes regarding their father. Yet she had. And now, in fact, she was gratefully teaming with her tracking down that very same Morgan Wickett. Was that horrid old pedophile really up to his sinful behaviors? All Pfot knew was that a girl at the kibbutz had been attacked by an unknown human assailant and had now gone missing. Mili was waiting on the porch when he pulled up. He got out, greeted her, and opened a back car door for her.

Mili smiled at her sister and observed that her Mardie's face was a bit flushed.

"Morning," she said. "Or should I say morning delight?"

"Is it that obvious?"

"In a word, yes. In a few words, it sure as Hell is. Good for you."

"Well, thank you. I am having more sex at age sixty-eight than I had when I was a youngster in school."

"Are you sure?" Mili asked. "Seems like you were flushed all the time back then."

"No, I really am doing it more now, I'm sure."

"Personally, I'm not setting any records," Mili confided. She frowned just thinking about it.

"Between the results of the bowling match and the disappearance of Brigitte, Lucifer doesn't sleep, doesn't eat, and doesn't et cetera either."

"Well, I'm sorry for that," Mardie said. "I don't think I could stay sane down here without the distractions of writing, the reenactment club, and getting laid on a regular basis."

"Language," Mili chided.

"What?" Mardie protested.

"*Getting laid* is a bit blue collar."

"Then make all my collars blue. Getting it on is probably the best thing two people can do."

Mili didn't respond.

"What?" Mardie asked again.

"I just realized that you're right. And not having that bond, that pleasure, can drive weak individuals to experience it forcibly."

"Like the man in the orchard, whoever he is."

"I know who I'd prefer that he isn't," Mili said. "Are you afraid of having to deal with Father again?"

"No," Mardie replied defiantly. "And if I have to, I'll deal with him exactly the way I dealt with him before." She opened her bag and pulled out a knife with a seven- or eight-inch blade.

"Dear God," Mili uttered. "You'd stab him again?"

"He just *looks* at me wrong and he's dead meat."

"That's murder down here, you know. Just like on Earth."

"No. It's called getting what's coming to you," Mardie said.

"You'd plead that before Lucifer?"

"You think I could claim self-defense?"

"Depends on how many times you stab him."

"I'll keep that in mind."

"It would be better just to keep your knife in your purse."

Mardie gazed at her sister for a long moment, then put the knife away.

"I never carried any kind of weapon when I was at the Yard," Mili said. "I never got threatened by anyone with a weapon. And I was never wounded in any way."

"I think my circumstances were different than yours."

"Of course they were."

"And I'm still glad I brought a knife now."

The trip took almost two hours. Pfot tried to avoid the worst of the bumps, ruts, and holes in the road, but it was a losing battle. The road was a mess. At 9:20 a.m. he was cleared to enter the kibbutz by the guards at the main gate, and they radioed ahead to tell David Ben-Gurion that the Wickett sisters were on their way up to the kibbutz.

Pfot pulled the Volvo up to the library and jumped out. He opened the car doors for Mili and Mardie. David Ben-Gurion walked up looking tired and irritated.

"Shalom," he said to Mili and shook her hand. He greeted Mardie and acknowledged Pfot with a wave of his hand.

"How bad is the news?" Mili asked.

"There's no news," Ben-Gurion told her. "The search parties were out most of the night, and after only a couple of hours of sleep, most folks have gone back out, combing and re-combing the orchards."

"Mardie and I are ready to help," Mili said. "I'd like to focus on the orchard area where Brigitte was originally attacked."

"We've been over that ground many times. Nothing."

"I understand. But I might see things that others missed."

"Fair enough. Ready to go now? It's not far from here."

Mili looked at her sister.

"Mardie?"

"I'm ready," she replied.

Mardie nodded. She was wearing jeans and a blue work shirt. Mili was wearing jeans as well, and a white tank top. Both women had sturdy shoes, having anticipated a walkabout in the fields where the citrus trees flourished. Ben-Gurion led the way into the orchards that bordered the kibbutz's dormitories and public buildings. The ground under the orange trees had been leveled and planted with herbs, plants, and tobacco.

"Those are for medicinal uses," Ben-Gurion said as he walked. Mardie spotted marijuana plants in the mix. Different strokes for different folks. If she felt poorly in the hours ahead she would ask specifically for a prescription from this spot.

"Why was Brigitte allowed to return to work by herself?" Mili asked.

"She wanted to stay busy," Ben-Gurion answered. "But her mood was so foul I couldn't find anyone willing to work with her. So she went off alone. I assigned field hands to bring in her filled crates and asked them to keep an eye on her without making it obvious."

"Alas, that effort was in vain," Mili commented. "Brigitte disappeared anyway."

"Yes. And I, among others, think she may have left on her own," David told her..

"If she left, did she take anything from her room?" she asked.

"We checked. Couldn't tell if she took any clothes or personal effects."

"By the field hands' reckoning," Mili asked, "when did they pick up the last full crates of oranges from her work area?"

"They made a collection at 4:30 p.m. and there were a half-dozen full crates waiting. At 5:30, the last collection of the day, there were no full crates."

"Were any crates partially filled, as if she'd been interrupted?"

"No," Ben-Gurion answered. "That is one of the things that makes many of us believe her exit was planned. She finished as much work as she intended to do and then left before it was dark."

"To go where?"

Ben-Gurion held his hands out as if to say, who knows?

Mardie looked up. My God. She hadn't noticed until now, but the skies above were blue with nary a cloud. She looked at Ben-Gurion and then at Mili.

"What's wrong with the sky?" she asked.

"The sky is blue here," Mili told her.

"Not supposed to be," was Mardie's lame response.

"Well, it is," Mili assured her. "Further, the water is sweet, the trees are healthy, and the kibbutz grows perfect fruit and vegetables."

"We do," Ben-Gurion responded. "Some three tons of food leave the kibbutz every day."

Mardie looked at Ben-Gurion's clothes. Plain black slacks, short-sleeve white shirt, black belt, and black shoes. He dressed in the same outfit every day. Didn't he have any money? She'd also noticed that the rows of Spartan dormitories were nothing more than utilitarian cinderblock buildings. Maybe nobody had any money around this place. She decided to ask David.

"What does the kibbutz do with the money it makes? It doesn't look like anyone's been on a spending spree."

"Every member of the kibbutz receives a share of the profits, though the largest percentage supports purchasing, maintaining, and adding to our vehicles, farm equipment, irrigation systems, modern drugs, and medical technology." Ben-Gurion paused and his eyes twinkled. "*And* to purchase food preferences imported from Earth that we enjoy, but don't grow or make here. Those items include beef and lamb, fresh fish and chicken, beer, wine, and schnapps.

"Plus, there is a continuing and significant amount of money needed to pay *and* bribe the demon suppliers who—though already charging a premium for their services—are delighted with any extra money they can extort. All in all, though, we invest those monies to both their and our satisfaction."

"A non zero sum situation," Mili suggested.

Ben-Gurion shook his head.

"Not quite. There are no win-wins in Hell. At least not officially. The demons always have a complaint to express, or a bone to pick. What we do have is a *mostly* balanced partnership with them, which for Hell is quite unusual. It works well enough."

Somewhere in the midst of hundreds of wonderful smelling orange trees Ben-Gurion stopped.

"Brigitte's work area began here and continued about fifty yards ahead and twenty-five yards or so in either direction."

"That seems like a lot of area for one person," Mardie remarked.

"Well, actually not," Ben-Gurion corrected her. "That's about 250 mature trees and they are pruned to keep their canopies low enough to pick their fruit using a small step ladder. Plus, not all the fruit on a given tree is ripe for picking any given day. Brigitte, being a competent and dedicated worker, could easily have handled this share of the orchard."

Mili felt saturated with orange orchard logistics.

"Let's talk about what we're looking for here," she said. "If Brigitte was taken by force there will be noticeable signs in the garden growth beneath the trees. Crushed plants or greenery trampled and ripped up. Those kinds of clues might reveal what happened to her. Or if we find clear indications that a patch of ground has been dug up and replaced, it will likely reveal that Brigitte was not kidnapped, but murdered and buried. What we are looking for may appear as a small mound if the digger settled for a shallow grave. It might also appear as flattened earth if he was careful to disguise his digging, but it will still show as freshly turned soil nonetheless."

Mardie pointed at something nearby.

"What?" Mili asked, irritated at being interrupted.

"There is place over there that looks exactly like what you're describing."

Mardie started off toward the spot. The others followed. No more than twenty steps away was an orange tree where the soil near its trunk had obviously been dug up and somewhat carelessly thrown back in. Plants were cut down and bits and pieces protruded from the tossed soil. There was also a distinct swell to the replaced dirt. Maybe five or six inches high. Everyone stared at the small mound of earth. Mardie had led them to the exact place where nothing could explain its appearance except a dead girl shoved in a hole and covered back up.

Mili got down on her knees and began clearing away the loose soil. Sweeping her hand gently back and forth across the dirt, she systematically swept off several inches and stopped when she touched something. Or someone. She used her forefinger to carefully push bits of dirt away, revealing a nose, a forehead, then cheeks and a mouth. She moved the soil very slowly and uncovered two dirt-encrusted eyes.

Mili reached into her purse for her handkerchief and pointed at the water canteen clipped to Ben-Gurion's belt. He handed it to her. She unscrewed the cap and poured water onto the handkerchief. She dabbed at the face and eyes until they were clean. Mili, Mardie, and Ben-Gurion gazed upon Brigitte's dead face, her open eyes and expression revealing her last moments alive. She had died terrified.

No one spoke. Then Mardie got on her knees and helped Mili clear away the rest of the soil heaped over Brigitte's body. She was naked. Her clothes had been tossed in the grave before she was put into it. Her vaginal area was full of caked blood, and her neck had been slit with a knife, her knife. Then stuck in her chest where it penetrated her heart.

Mardie felt faint and sat down on the ground. Mili stood up and brushed her hands off. She shook her head. No one should ever have had to experience this. Not this girl. Not any female. Mardie had once been attacked. But she had survived. Brigitte had not. She had been raped and murdered. Goddammit. What kind of place was Hell turning into?

CHAPTER SIXTEEN

Ben-Gurion spoke softly.

"I will call for help. A four-wheel-drive vehicle can be brought to carry her body back."

"Not yet, David," Mili said. "Before we move her body, I need to examine it and reconstruct as best I can what might have happened."

Ben-Gurion nodded and stood back.

Mili carefully examined Brigitte's wounds first. She wet her handkerchief again and began to clean the cut across Brigitte's neck. It was a clean cut, done quickly and without resistance. Mili picked up one of Brigitte's wrists. No marks. She had not been tied. She looked at Brigitte's chest. There was a large bloodless mark in the center, likely the result of the assailant holding her down with his knee.

She had bled to death so quickly there wasn't time for a bruise to form. The mark was deep and the skin had been torn and shredded. Mili imagined the man holding her down and swiftly slitting her neck, and while she watched in horror he plunged the knife into her naked chest. There was very little blood pooled around the knife wound. The dagger thrust had likely pierced Brigitte's heart making her death almost instantaneous.

Mili cleaned the blood and dirt from the vaginal area. The tissue was raw and filthy. The assailant had used his dirty hands to push her legs open and forced himself on her so violently that the inner walls of her vagina were torn. Mili turned and looked at Mardie. Her sister was sitting with her head between her legs. Mili gently lifted up the cadaver's torso and gazed at Brigitte's back. It was soiled by the dirt, but free of wounds. She laid the body down again, closed Brigitte's eyes, and stood up.

Without being asked, Ben-Gurion unbuttoned his white shirt and took it off. He handed it to Mili who laid it over Brigitte's bare torso. At least one indignity had been addressed.

Mili pulled her mobile phone out of her purse. It was a half hour shy of noon. Lucifer should be at his office. Before she could punch in his number, Mardie shrieked. Mili jerked her head up. Mardie's outstretched arm was pointing toward the heart of the orchard. A single orange tree had flamed up like a torch. Then several more trees exploded into flame, fire ripping up their trunks and engulfing the branches.

"Someone has doused the trees with gas or kerosene!" Ben-Gurion cried and ran straight for the flaming trees. Mili knew that the arsonist would see Ben-Gurion and flee. That wouldn't make any difference though in terms of saving the grove. It was lost. The flames jumped tree to tree and swept straight toward where she and Mardie were standing.

They had walked into the orchard from the kibbutz, but they would perish now unless they ran hard. They would have to leave Brigitte's body. One more humiliation the poor girl had to face. Cremated while lying in her own grave. But there was no choice. The wind was driving the fire right at them.

"Run!" Mili cried. And Mardie did. As she and Mili fled the flames, a score of bladed Caterpillars appeared and began pushing up a protective dirt wall between the collective's buildings and the blazing orange grove. The fire spread to all the citrus trees in the orchard, and then onto thousands of others. By early evening, all of the kibbutz's citrus groves had been destroyed.

Mili and Mardie had watched the conflagration along with thousands of the men and women who lived on the kibbutz. There was weeping, grieving, and murmurs of sadness as they watched the work of generations of kibbutzniks turn to ash.

David Ben-Gurion returned and sought out Mili and Mardie. He was furious.

"The man who killed Brigitte burned down our groves to cover up his crime," he spit out. "Heartless bastard."

"His efforts will prove futile," Mili said. "I promise you. As large and anonymous as Hell seems, there are files on everyone who dwells here, and I think I already have a suspect of interest. He can hide. He can burn the evidence. But he will not escape justice. Hell only has so many nooks and crannies, and whichever one the beast has chosen to inhabit, I will flush him out."

David Ben-Gurion stared at Mili, speechless after hearing her solemn vow.

"She'll do it," Mardie told him, putting her hand on his arm. "She's unstoppable. Trust me."

Ben-Gurion gazed at Mili and Mardie.

"I had no idea you girls were Jewish."

* * *

Mili and Mardie sat in Moshe Dayan's one-room apartment with both him and Ben-Gurion. Their togetherness provided a feeling of safety and respite from the horrors of the day. Moshe's bachelor space was filled with Holy Land antiquities of all kinds—clay oil lamps, terracotta storage jars, bronze statues, and mosaic panels.

Moshe's decorating was as arresting as his strange and beautiful treasures. He had a nice gold-colored leather sofa and several olivewood chairs that he had made himself. There were gorgeous carpets from India and bookshelves filled with books and miniature glass vessels from Phoenicia, Rome, and Egypt. Moshe served everyone sweetened iced tea in tall colorful Moroccan glasses. He and his guests sat and talked, comforted by each other's presence.

"Where did you get all these old pieces?" Mardie asked. "Some of them are pretty creepy."

Moshe smiled, amused at Mardie's reaction.

"They're all pieces from my collection," Moshe explained. "I had them brought down by demon services."

"What Moshe isn't telling you," Ben-Gurion interjected, "is that he dug all over Israel without permits and kept what he liked."

"And every last piece got donated to the Israeli Museum," Moshe responded, offended. Ben-Gurion swept his arm around the room. "Well, almost every piece then," Moshe snapped and crossed his arms over his chest, clearly upset.

Mili got up and pointed at a small metal figure on Moshe's work desk. "May I?" she asked.

"Of course," Moshe answered. "Please be careful. It is more than four thousand years old."

Mili picked up the figure, an upright human body with a bull's head complete with long curving horns. She studied it for a moment.

"The Minotaur?" she guessed. "Skulking around in the labyrinth beneath King Minos'
palace."

"Indeed," Moshe said, nodding approvingly. "You might be surprised to know that the creature was actually a son of Minos and a concubine from his palace harem. The bull's head was a leather mask and virgins sent to Minos as tribute were ritually deflowered by the Minotaur, in front of his father, the king, and his drunken courtiers."

"What an awful story," Mili said disgusted. "Yet once again proving that every myth holds a grain of truth…" her voice trailed off.

136

"A grain that is—more often than not—completely abhorrent," Ben-Gurion said.

"How do you know that any of what you just told us is true?" Mili asked Moshe.

"How do you think?" Moshe asked, turning the question back on Mili.

"Oh God," Mili uttered and just stared at Moshe. "You *talked* to him."

Moshe nodded.

"I talk to everybody. Archaeology digs up more than old junk. Down here in Hell I've searched out the great figures of human history, be they famous or infamous, and heard them tell the stories of their adventures. Every heinous villain, every cruel god, and every evil entity is down here, and more than happy to be recognized."

"Was the Minotaur's fetish," Mili asked, "the ritual rape of virgins, a common practice among the aberrants whom you questioned?"

"Every one of them."

"What?" Mili cried in disbelief.

"Not every figure steeped in infamy managed to indulge in such lustful desires, but most characters with power or wealth—from the Minotaur to the Libyan dictator Muammar Gaddafi—savaged virgins both in public rituals and private indulgences, beating, mutilating, raping, and even killing the victims."

"I thought I had just one suspect," Mili said quietly. "Now I find that Hell is bulging with candidates. Shit. Piss. Fuck."

Both Ben-Gurion and Moshe Dayan were surprised at Mili's language, but only because of its contrast with her usual elegant and intellectual demeanor. It was, however, far from the worst that they had ever heard. Female Israeli's in the kibbutz could swear circles around Mili having learned how to curse during their mandatory hitch in the army. And Mardie herself could pop off vulgarities at ten times Mili's rate just while having sex.

"Mili," Mardie spoke up. "Don't you find it curious that none of Moshe's list of legendary predators have ever indulged in their violent behaviors down here?"

"No," Mili answered. "Such conduct would have subjected any such perpetrator to torture and disfigurement. No hands. No feet. No penis. Who wants to live like that for the rest of eternity?"

"So why then do we suddenly have someone who is willing to risk that kind of disfigurement?" Mardie countered.

"Because that criminal is delusional," Ben-Gurion answered for Mili. "He either believes that he will never be captured, *or* his sins on Earth were so heinous that he actually yearns to be caught and disfigured, finally paying the price for what he did *before* he was damned."

Mili sat silently and ran those two scenarios through her brain. The first portrait was of a man living in a fantasy world where he believed he would not be found. That could be any psychopath in Hell. The second description was of a man agonized by his guilt and wanting to be punished, and that could also describe a wide swath of Hell's male population.

Mili wasn't sure that either condition applied to Morgan Wickett, however. She was more inclined to think that he was satisfying his lust with no real thought about his victims or the horrendous punishment he'd receive when he was caught. That had happened before when he ran into a blade that stopped him when he hadn't stopped himself. Whatever the truth, he had to be tracked down and apprehended immediately. There was no sand left to fall to the bottom of her hour glass.

* * *

Pfotenhauer drove Mili and Mardie home. After dinner, Little Mardie went to her room to play video games. Video games down here were manufactured by gaming companies on Earth expressly ordered for game junkies in Hell. No one making them knew that and they certainly would have denied the existence of any such demographic if they'd been told. Demon network be thanked.

Silicon Valley twenty-something programmers thought the portrayal of Hell as specified was seriously juvenile. Gray skies, scorched earth, urban wreckage. None of the brainy developers from Stanford thought Hell was like that, but the designer's requirements were very clear about what Hell should look like and how it should appear in the game's setting.

Creating fat demons cracked up the gamers, and illustrating dimwitted Shapeshifters cracked them up even more. And when the Biblical reenactments needed coding, the software engineers laughed so hard they had trouble using their keyboards.

Sooner or later, however, playable videos were created, manufactured in China, and brought to Hell. Fans down here had tons of video games to choose from. Most had to do with drinking, drugs, sex, plastic surgery, and religious reenactments. The games weren't rated as there were no children in Hell except for Little Mardie, and Mili carefully screened her daughter's want list before approving which games would be purchased.

As soon as Little Mardie had left the dinner table to play her games, Mili asked Lucifer if she could fill him in on her case. Satan was very interested to learn what she was up to. In her first case down here, she had brilliantly tracked down a murderer who had entered Hell through a hole in space. Lucifer had figured then that there wouldn't be any more cases for her after that. Wrong, He drank the black coffee Mili set before him and waited for her to start. She sat with her own cup of tea amply laced with cream and sugar and presented the first and ugliest detail right at the start.

"The man who assaulted the young girl at the farm collective returned last night, raped and killed her."

Satan stared at Mili, shocked at her words.

"It can't be."

"It can be," Mili said, "and it is. And I believe that the man who did it was my father."

Lucifer sat speechless.

"He began this pattern of evil behavior on Earth. For whatever reason he has chosen to resume it down here."

Lucifer shook his head.

"Stupid bastard. We'll find him and cut his member off. And then his arms and legs."

"Some haste *is* necessary, Lu. The man was and is a pedophile who attacked and forced himself on the victim down here because of her slightness and girlish appearance."

Lucifer scowled, his face full of anger and vengeance.

"Are you suggesting that he would dare to approach my daughter? His own granddaughter?"

A host of flames appeared on his head, shoulders, and arms.

"We need to deny him the opportunity," Mili said. "I need you to mobilize your demons. Every business, every store, every home in Hell has to be searched. Now."

"I'm on it," Lucifer roared and stood up. He flamed into a small sun forcing Mili to step back from the intense heat. In a moment her husband flamed out and returned to his own shape. He gave Mili a peck on the cheek, then walked to the kitchen door that led outside. He turned and looked at Mili. "Watch Little Mardie. I will surround the house with an army of Samn demons and dispatch devils to every corner of Hell to find your father.

"When apprehended, he shall be tortured, maimed, and consumed by fire. And Mili, my love, this will be the last time I ever acknowledge that man as your biological parent. From now on, he's just Morgan Wickett. Dead man walking."

CHAPTER SEVENTEEN

ili stayed at home with Little Mardie while Lucifer turned Hell upside down. Every mobile phone had a picture of Morgan Wickett on its screen, as did every television, cable, and public monitor saying that he was wanted for murder and rape. Every website in Hell carried images of his face, and Lucifer posted a ten-million-dollar reward for information that led to Wickett's discovery and arrest.

Mardie sat at her kitchen table drinking tea and staring at the picture of her father on her phone screen. He had a long face and a short, trimmed beard, without a moustache. His black hair was thick and unruly. At first glance many folks who saw him on Earth thought he looked like Abraham Lincoln.

But Morgan Wickett's hooded eyes were steely and dark, putting off strangers from approaching him and reminding his only acquaintances—fellow workers at the small iron forge where he was employed and drinkers he sat with at the pub—that something fearful and savage lay deep within the quiet man.

She didn't know when and where Lucifer had found the photograph. Didn't matter if it was taken of Morgan Wickett bound for Hell or Morgan Wickett entering Hell, she would not forget the emotionless face attached to the lanky body that had taken her night after night as a young teenager, finishing with urgency and grunts like a pig.

Until the night she'd said no and struggled to push his naked body off of hers. He roared like a madman and began hitting her face and her breasts with his fists, calling her foul names and cursing her as though she represented every woman who had ever spurned him. He penetrated her again, crushing himself hard against her. She reached for the knife she'd hidden under her pillow and plunged it into his neck. Without a sound he sagged and rolled onto the floor.

Her father lay on his back, speechless, pressing his hand against the artery emptying the blood out of his body. And then it was over. Eyes frozen, lungs flat, heart stopped. Three unimpeachable witnesses that Morgan Wickett had truly expired. Mardie and two blokes had disposed of the body, burying it just inside the boundary of Nottingham Forest. No one ever found him. No one ever questioned her. And despite the years of abuse and trauma climaxed by their last struggle and his murder, Mardie very rarely thought again about the monster who had been her da.

When her sister Mili had found out that Mardie had killed him, it had caused a bitter divide between them. In time, Mili accepted the crime for what it truly was, Mardie's struggle to survive without being subject to rape and abuse, and held Mardie blameless. But God hadn't. She wound up in Hell and so had Morgan Wickett. And now the man she never wanted to see again had all of Hell looking for him.

Mardie tried to think of something else. It was not to be. Heavy knocking at her door startled her so much she dropped her tea cup on the kitchen rug. She picked it up. Someone pounded on her door again. She looked through the peep hole. Two large, scarlet Samn demons looked back. She unlocked the door and opened it.

"Mardell Wickett?" one of the demons inquired in a gruff voice.

"Yes."

"We are authorized by Lord Lucifer to search your house for this man." The demon stuck an enlargement of Morgan Wickett's face in front of her eyes.

The Samn's eyes narrowed.

"You have the same last name as the suspect," he almost hissed.

"No relation."

"How can I be sure?"

"You can't. Write my name down and call Satan."

"Are you being a smart ass?"

"Not any more than usual."

"Well, I don't like it."

"Well, I don't like you."

The Samn reared his head back, insulted.

"How about if you just do your damn job?" Mardie suggested.

The Samn began to shout.

"How would you like to be taken to Lord Lucifer himself?"

"Fine," Mardie answered. "He'd probably be glad to see me. Maybe even ask me to judge how you performed your duties." Mardie looked into the demon's golden lion eyes. "He's married to my sister."

The Samn froze instantly, as if Mardie had nailed him with a Dungeons and Dragons cone of coldness. The other Samn stood silent.

"All right," Mardie said. "Go ahead and check the house. 'Course the perp you're looking for isn't here, but I respect that you have to look."

In less than three minute, the Samns had searched rooms, closets, drawers, and under the beds. Mr. I'm-so-sorry-I-made-you-upset bowed and exited without a word out the open front door. The other Samn, the quiet one, paused at the doorsill and spoke to Mardie.

"I noticed that you had an undersized dildo in your bedside stand. If you'd like something bigger, call me. I texted you my name and number."

"You've got some balls," Mardie said, entertained.

"Actually I don't have any balls," the demon responded. "But I do have this." The red skin between his naked legs parted like some sort of sea creature's secret vault and out came an erect rose-colored penis at least eighteen inches long.

"I've never had sex with a devil before," Mardie said in awe. "Are all of you built that way?"

"Only Samns to my knowledge."

"Have you ever had sex with an Earth woman?" Mardie asked.

"No. But I think I just found one who will make that happen." Mardie snorted.

"You're confident," she said.

"I'd rather be lucky," the demon replied.

"Well, maybe that too," Mardie answered. She watched as the Samn's exposed organ withdrew. He smiled at her coyly. Holden Caulfield hoping to catch her in the rye. She smiled, then kissed the demon on the cheek and closed the door. Then again, she thought, the hopeful demon might *not* score. She'd never made love to a baseball bat before.

Mardie washed her tea cup, then refilled it and sat at the table. She took a sip. It was just warm enough to be comforting. She took another sip and called Mili.

"Guess who just rousted up my house?"

"Demons in search of you-know-who," Mili answered.

"Yep. Samn demons. I've been pretty scared of them ever since one threatened to tear my arms off for being sassy."

"I've noticed that you often have that effect on males."

"One of them flirted with me. Gave me a glimpse of his concealed weapon."

"No!" Mili cried.

"Yes. Rod the length of a ruler and a lot more."

"Probably be more painful than having your arms torn off."

"That occurred to me," Mardie agreed. "Plus, I'd have a whole new opening in my lower back."

"Okay, stop. Did anyone search your house or just your interest?"

"There were two demons and they looked everywhere. One ran into the dildo in my bed stand and that's what turned him on."

"Since when do you need a dildo with Bowles frequenting the premises?" Mili asked.

"Ever since I put together a first-aid kit for the house."

"Ha! I take it the Samns are gone?"

"Yes, but there are dozens outside," Mardie replied. "Your husband must have mobilized a zillion of them."

"Then I pray they capture Dad."

"He's not my dad," Mardie protested. "He's a fucker who took my body and almost my life. If I had not acted first I'd be dead and gone, just like Brigitte at the kibbutz."

"Do you really think he would have killed you?"

"Yes."

"Lucifer has threatened to torture him and then burn him alive," Mili told her.

"Horrible. I'll light the match."

"Understandable."

"Seeing the Samn's naked member made me think about a few things," Mardie went on.

"Do I want to hear them?" Mili responded.

"Yes. They're detective kinds of things."

"Okay."

"Who do demons have sex with?"

"I never thought about it," Mili said slowly. "I assumed other demons."

"It's worth considering that most demons are male," Mardie noted. "So maybe Basts service them. Or Earth women down here. On the other hand, I doubt any female, demon or human, would take on a Samn because of the size of its sex organ. I'm telling you, Mili, I hurt just seeing that devil's tool.

"Now just suppose the rapist is a demon who cannot get women in Hell to do him. He spots the female at the kibbutz, Brigitte, all by herself, and decides he will risk everything to have sex with her. He attacks her twice and succeeds the second time, literally ripping up her lady parts. Then he burns the citrus groves down to destroy the body along with the evidence. A physical assault that would have revealed she had been raped by a demon and not by a human."

"A troubling accusation," Mili replied, "but muted by the fact that when Brigitte is restored to a new Hellion body she may be able to identify her assailant."

"I'm not so sure you should count on that," Mardie replied. "Have you heard one word from your husband about any plans he has to go to God and request her Hellion replacement?"

"No, but he has to. It's divine law."

"But if Lucifer thinks there is a chance that a demon committed the crime—something that he perhaps he doesn't want the Almighty to learn about—he might at the very least *delay* his request until things get resolved down here."

"You're treading on forbidden ground," Mili said, feeling anxious listening to Mardie's scenario. "And you are theorizing at the expense of my husband."

"I don't mean to do that, sis," Mardie apologized, "not at all. Maybe seeing that Samn expose himself got me thinking all the wrong kinds of things."

Mili did not respond. Mardie's suggestions were painful to hear and worse to ponder. Imagining Lucifer bending justice for a demon was unthinkable, yet Mardie had just made that very accusation. She'd made her sister apologize, but that didn't make her words go away. The truth would come out, Mili knew that, but perhaps in ways that would threaten the ruler of Hell and his family along with it.

※ ※ ※

The house by house, building by building, search for Morgan Wickett continued through the day, spreading out across Hell from New Babylon. Homes and shops in every city and town were scoured, and by the end of the day each farm and farming enterprise in rural areas had been hunted through as well.

Mili was afraid that when demons reported to Lucifer the amazing phenomena they'd observed on the kibbutz, the Devil might have some questioning for *her*. She called Ben-Gurion to get a feel as to how the demons had reacted when they saw the kibbutz.

"Milicent!" Ben-Gurion declared, picking up the call. "How are you, dear?"

"I am feeling somewhat desperate, to be frank," she admitted. "The man suspected of murdering Brigitte is still at large. He is somehow eluding the legions of demons my husband sent looking for him."

"An inspection team was here this morning," David said. "More like a pack really. A dozen or so misshapen devils crisscrossed the kibbutz looking in dormitories, equipment sheds, and private domiciles. They even searched the thousands of acres of nut trees and produce gardens, which are the only agricultural areas that didn't burn last night. I have to say that they were respectful and some of them were actually familiar with our co-op as they'd heard of our wonderful fruits and vegetables."

"Did they note anything else?"

"They noted *everything* else. They commented on the blue skies, the acres of flowers,
the healthy trees, the vibrant plants, even the dark, rich soil. Several expressed sympathy over the loss of the citrus groves, and I have to tell you that even tough old Moshe was touched."

"I have to say that I am, too." Mili's low opinion of demons rose slightly. "Do you think they will report back to Lucifer about what they witnessed?"

"No. Since other demons are involved in moving our produce, these Samns will not betray those business relationships. Besides,"

Ben-Gurion paused and winked at Mili, "we lined the pockets of the chaps who were here and asked for discretion concerning what they had witnessed."

"I don't suppose you lined their pockets with broccoli or Brussels sprouts?"

"Ho, ho!" Ben-Gurion laughed. "You are quite charming. And the answer is no. We lined their pockets with cash."

"You bribed them."

"Absolutely. When in Hell, do as the Hellions do."

Mili grinned.

"Should we be lining your pockets, too?" Ben-Gurion asked.

"Asparagus would be best."

David nodded pleased.

"By the way, your own secret is safe with us."

Mili frowned.

"What secret would that be?"

"Your ice cream franchise," Ben-Gurion answered. "The Mammon who made the loan has sort of a big mouth."

"Dear God!"

"Yes, and we're all praying to the good Lord that you'll open a Ben and Jerry's store here on the kibbutz."

"I thought you didn't believe in God."

"Listen, Mili, to get a cold scoop of pistachio ice cream down here I'd believe in Allah."

Mili grinned and shook her head.

"Good luck on the manhunt," Ben-Gurion said turning serious. "I have to share that I felt concern for you when I saw that the last name of the man on the poster was Wickett."

Mili didn't respond. What would be the point of revealing to even such a kind and understanding person as David Ben-Gurion that the prime suspect was her own father?

"If I may," David said tenderly, "allow me say that it is no reflection on you what any other Wickett may *or may not* have done. You are you, and that's all that matters to your friends."

"That Wickett is my father, David. He hurt my sister when we were growing up."

Ben-Gurion frowned.

"So the man has a hard history. That's sad, and I am sorry for you and your sister. But his sins are his own, and so are the consequences of his actions."

Mili felt tears rising.

"Thank you, David. I have to go and cry now."

"You do that, Mili. Please know that I am always here when you want to talk."

Mili ended the call and cried, as long and hard as she could ever remember. For herself,

for her sister, and for her father. Her tears were laden with the emotional toxins welling up from all the sadness she had ever carried for her poor ruin of a family.

Then she washed her face and went to check on Little Mardie who'd been playing Hell videos all day. She'd be lucky if her daughter hadn't somehow found a way to enter into those gruesome games, wreaking havoc on the forces of darkness, fighting robot vampires, destroying cyborg werewolves, and banishing demi-god necromancers. Thank heavens that such horrendous creatures were mere electronic figments of some perverse game designer's mind.

On the other hand, she had never heard of any of those hybrid beasties raping and killing a woman no larger than a teenage girl. Said a lot about who the real abominations were.

CHAPTER EIGHTEEN

L ittle Mardie?" Mili called, walking up the stairs to her daughter's room. The door was shut. She knocked and called again. "Little Mardie?" She opened the door and looked in the room. Little Mardie was not there. Mili checked both upstairs bathrooms. No Little Mardie.

Mili scowled and tried to remember when her daughter might have snuck past her. When she sat at the table crying? No. She hadn't been that oblivious. There must be a space hole somewhere up here. An escape Little Mardie had used before.

She had to call Lucifer and share the news. Not a good day for Little Mardie to decide to wander around on her own. She got her husband on his private mobile number.

"Hi there," Lucifer answered.

Mili got right to the point.

"Is there a wormhole somewhere upstairs in our house?"

"Yes," Satan answered, a little unnerved at his wife's directness.

"One you've known about and didn't bother to tell me?" Mili snapped.

"An oversight, sorry."

"Yet at some point you told Little Mardie about it, correct?"

"Don't remember that. More likely she saw me use it."

"To go where?"

"Straight to Avalon Lanes."

"And where is the hole?"

"In the master bathroom. In the corner by the scale."

"So, I could have fallen into it just weighing myself?"

"Maybe," Lucifer answered slowly. "You have to put a hand or a foot inside the opening to use it."

"Well, your daughter evidently put her hand in and then the rest of herself. She's not here."

The Devil looked stunned.

"She left today—of all days—without telling you?" Lucifer was panicking. "I'll have Pfotenhauer pick you up while I go to Avalon Lanes and search for her. Meet me there."

"Do you have another secret hole at headquarters?"

"No. I'm going to run like hell."

Mili's fears skyrocketed as her worries for Little Mardie took hold. How could her daughter have done this? As the only teenager in Hell her grandfather would surely know who she was. Had he stalked her? Did he know her routines? Followed her when she was alone? Learned to recognize her long walks downtown to shop or dine at one of her favorite places?

Dear God, why hadn't she thought about this before now? Probably because she hadn't had to. This was Hell. Little Mardie was the daughter of Hell's ruler. There was no person in Hell safer than her daughter. Until Brigitte had been assaulted and killed. Mili's mind raced as she went downstairs and waited on the porch for Pfot to arrive.

Cursing herself with every foul Cockney insult she'd ever heard, she suddenly realized that Little Mardie had to be carrying her cell phone. Mili yanked her own phone out of her purse and punched in her daughter's mobile number. Little Mardie's face appeared on the screen.

"I know, I know," her daughter said immediately. "I'm in big trouble for leaving without telling you."

Mili could have collapsed with relief at the sight of her daughter's face.

"I'm more concerned that you're all right," she responded. "Haven't you seen the pictures the demons are carrying around everywhere? The man they are searching for is a very dangerous individual."

"I've seen the pictures," Little Mardie replied, "and I haven't seen that person. However, I have met a man who claims he's my grandfather. He seems pretty nice."

Mili froze. She could barely whisper her next question.

"Are you at the bowling alley?"

"Yes."

"And he's with you? Don't let him know I'm on the phone with you, honey. He is *not* nice. Do not under any circumstances let him talk you into leaving with him."

"Mother, I don't think we're talking about the same person." Little Mardie turned her phone toward the man sitting at the table next her. "See?"

Mili did see. The man gazing at the camera was clean shaven and wearing a Frank Sinatra hat pulled low over his forehead. He didn't look anything like the picture the demons were circulating, but Mili had no doubt who was cozying up to her daughter. It was Morgan Wickett.

* * *

Pfotenhauer reached Avalon Lanes at record speeds. He averaged more than seventy miles an hour on Hell's terrible arterials, delivering a bone-jarring ride for Mili and the worst stress test of its long and honorable career for Satan's Volvo. Mili ran into the bowling alley and discovered Lucifer shouting at the Samn demons who worked there.

"You saw her sitting at a table with an older man and you didn't investigate?" Satan hollered at the top of his archangelic voice. Both scarlet-skinned Samn demons shrank back from Satan's ferocious wrath. "What's the matter with you two idiots?"

"The man did not match the description of the person we were searching for," one muttered, fear in his voice.

"So you just ignored the fact that my daughter was *with someone you didn't know* because he didn't look like the criminal we're searching for all over Hell?"

Both Samns lowered their heads and didn't answer.

"Tell me when you noticed that Little Mardie left?" Satan asked still furious.

"She didn't leave, Master," one Samn answered. "We didn't interrupt your daughter or her guest, but we did watch them. After you called to tell us you were coming, we saw that your daughter and the man she had been talking to had disappeared."

"You didn't see them leave?" Satan was yelling again.

"Beg pardon, Lord, but they didn't leave. We are sure of it."

"How can you two goddamn meat bags be sure of anything?" Flames shot up on Satan's scalp.

Mili arrived and stepped into the confrontation. She looked at Lucifer's face. He calmed down immediately.

"Lu, it's obvious that Little Mardie and her grandfather used the wormhole."

Satan looked horrified.

"The one that goes to San Francisco?"

"Yes. That one over there." She pointed to the spot where the end of the bar butted up against the wall.

"They've gone to Earth."

"We have to follow them!" Lucifer cried. "It's our only hope of saving our daughter."

Satan took his wife's hand and led her to the hole in space.

"Go!" Mili urged.

Lucifer stepped into the invisible opening in space and disappeared. Mili followed, knowing exactly where the hole would take them. What she didn't know was where Little Mardie had gone on the other side. At least she'd only had a half-hour head start.

✳ ✳ ✳

Mardie's mobile phone rang. She set her dish towel by the sink and picked it up. The ID said Paul Pfotenhauer was calling. That never happened unless he was coming to give her a ride. And she hadn't asked for one. Refusing to panic, she answered.

"Evening, Pfot," she spoke. "Let me sit down and then you can give me the bad news."

"I think you'd better."

Mardie sat down, her heart racing.

Pfot looked devastated.

"Little Mardie is missing," he told her. "She is likely with your father."

"Oh, my God," Mardie groaned. Only by her strength of will did she keep from falling off the chair and collapsing on the kitchen floor.

Pfot went on, speaking rapidly.

"Apparently he approached her at Avalon Lanes. He didn't look at all like the picture being circulated, and simply identified himself as her grandfather. The Samns at the alley saw them sitting and talking, and then they disappeared. Lord Lucifer and Mrs. Mili are persuaded that Little Mardie used the hole in the corner by the bar to go to San Francisco. The master and your sister have followed."

"How do you know any of this, Pfot?" Mili asked totally stressed.

"Mrs. Mili had me pick her up at home and drive her to the bowling alley to meet the Devil. She told me everything."

"Where are you now?"

"Standing outside your door."

"What?" Mardie muttered.

"I know how to find Little Mardie. May I come in?"

"Right now."

Mardie opened the door and found Pfot waiting.

"Thank you, Miss Mardie."

"Sit anywhere."

Mardie pointed at her living room. Pfot took a leather chair. Mardie sat in its twin next to him.

"Explain quickly, Pfot. Time is obviously precious."

"Yes, Miss. Not so long ago I suggested to Little Mardie that we connect on a mobile application where either one of us could find the other person's whereabouts just by checking it. Seemed liked a good idea since Little Mardie enjoys her freedom."

"And she agreed?"

"Yes, she did. We're linked."

"So we can find out where she's at on the other side?"

"Precisely."

"Let's go!"

Pfot drove Grand Prix style to Avalon Lanes for the second time in less than an hour, and without a word to the Samn demons at the alley he and Mardie went straight for the hole. Mardie stepped in. Pfot followed. They stepped out on top of a tall hill overlooking San Francisco. A brisk breeze whipped the summit.

"Does your mobile work?" Mardie asked Pfot immediately.

"Look up," he said. Above them rose a tall orange transmission tower. "Demons have added repeater and amplification hardware up there. Our phones will work here without any issues."

"Great," Mardie said, feeling hopeful for the first time since Pfot had called her. "See if you can locate Little Mardie while I call Mili."

Mili picked up instantly.

"Mardie? How can you be calling me?"

"Pfot and I are both here. He and Little Mardie have a location share feature. We can use it to locate her if she still has her phone."

"Dear God," Mili sighed deeply. "Thank you, Mardie, thank you! Lucifer and I are at Fisherman's Wharf. I came here once with Little Mardie. We thought she might have come back."

"And?"

"No luck."

Pfot tapped Mardie on the shoulder and held up his phone screen for her to see.

"Pfot's app says she's having breakfast at a pancake house," Mardie told Mili. "It's on Hayes Street near Octavia. Take a cab and we'll meet you there. Go, go, go."

Mili looked at Mardie's face for a moment longer.

"Thank you sis," she said. "Now GO!"

✳ ✳ ✳

Lucifer and Mili got to the restaurant first. Sheridan's Pancake House on Hayes Street. It was a small establishment with French windows in front.

"Call Pfotenhauer," Lucifer urged Mili.

Mili did, glad to be doing something other than feeling so worried she wanted to throw up.

"Hello, Mrs. Mili," Pfot answered.

"We're at the restaurant," Mili told her. "Is Little Mardie still in there?"

"Yes."

"I'm going to text her and let her know that we're here."

"Might be pretty risky for her to even look at her phone if Morgan is with her," Pfot said.

"I have to do it," she insisted, and switched off.

Mili texted her daughter. To her surprise Little Mardie texted back immediately.

"Hello, Mom."

"Prove you're my daughter," Mili texted.

"Dad doesn't know that you're the one opening the Ben and Jerry's ice cream shops."

Lucifer scowled when he saw that over Mili's shoulder and looked sharply at his wife.

"Not now!" she cried.

"Are you alone?" Mili texted.

"No, but Grandfather is using his phone."

"Are you okay?"

"Yes. And actually, I'm a little disappointed in you and Aunt Mardie. He told me about how you always ignored him when you were growing up and spent all your time with your mum."

Mili felt sick, but answered instantly.

"Little Mardie, honey, the truth is that he hurt your aunt terribly when she was your age, and she killed him for it."

"Oh, my God!"

"You're in great danger."

"I'm not afraid."

"He can hurt you, love!" Mili texted desperately. "Hurt you emotionally. Hurt you physically."

"I understand."

"If Morgan is on the level with you, then why has he been avoiding all of us?"

"He's afraid of Daddy."

"He's got worse troubles," Mili wrote. "Aunt Mardie is down here, too. The last time she saw him she stuck a knife in his neck."

Little Mardie didn't text back.

Mili held her breath and waited.

"We're here!" Mardie called out, running to where Mili and Lucifer were standing. "Is Little Mardie really in there?"

"Yes," Lucifer told her. "She's been texting Mili."

"And she's with Morgan?"

"He doesn't apparently know we're here."

Lucifer looked at his watch.

"It's been more than a minute since Little Mardie texted us," Mili said.

"We've waiting long enough," Lucifer responded. "I'm going in!"

CHAPTER NINETEEN

L ucifer swung open the restaurant door and entered. Everyone
followed. There were only a few diners. No Little Mardie. No
Morgan Wickett.

A host came up to them. He was a big, well-built man, with a
shaved head and a long beard, wearing tan slacks and a Hawaiian shirt.

Mili spoke up.

"We're late to meet my father and daughter. Have they left already?"

The big man smiled.

"Yes. He paid and they exited through the back."

Mili scowled and grit her teeth. There was a back exit? Fucking
nice work, Ms. Scotland Yard.

"Thank you. May we go out that way as well?" she asked.

"Sure."

The host pointed straight toward the back of the restaurant.

The door opened into an alley. No one was there.

"Pfot?" Mili cried.

He was already searching for Little Mardie's location.

"We have to go back around front. They're one street up on Olivia."

"Lead the way!" Mili commanded.

Pfot hurried around the restaurant, crossed the street, and cut left at the next one. He stopped in front of a large garage with a sliding wooden door.

"She's in there," he said simply. "The app says there's a workshop and a gallery behind that big door. It notes that it's also unlocked. If Little Mardie and Morgan are in there, other people may be in there as well."

"Only one way to find out," Lucifer said. He pulled open the sliding door. Inside were wooden curio cabinets filled with ethnic art. There was a workbench in one corner with a vice and tools. Standing next to the workbench was Morgan Wickett holding Little Mardie's hand.

"Well, it looks like a family reunion," Morgan said. His voice was soft and thin. "I have enjoyed getting to know Little Mardie, and despite these strange circumstances, I have to say that it's nice to see you Mili. And you, too, Mardie. It's been a long time."

Little Mardie looked calm. She smiled and looked directly at her mother. Then she winked. Mili frowned. She had no idea what her daughter meant by that.

Morgan stepped closer with Little Mardie in tow until less than six feet separated him from his twin daughters.

Mardie walked toward Morgan and confronted him.

"Did you tell your granddaughter about what kind of father you were to me?"

Morgan smiled, took off his small hat, and scratched the top of his head. He put his hat back on and replied.

"We haven't had time to chat about everything."

"So, no rape stories yet?" Mili said, her voice harsh and demanding.

"I never raped you," her father said. "It was never rape, sweet Mardie, was it?" Morgan looked calm and benevolent.

"You raped me, you son of a bitch!" Mardie screamed. "You took advantage of me and turned violent when I refused to be used anymore.

Then I killed you, *Father*. Killed you for your transgressions!" Mardie cried. "Or did you forget?"

"I didn't forget. You took my life, Mardie. I died in your arms." Morgan looked at his daughter and shook his head sadly.

Mili searched her father's neck. She looked for the scar her knife had left.

"So how did we get into this fracas?" Morgan asked reasonably.

"You fucking ran off with my daughter!" Satan bellowed.

"I did not. We met by accident at one of your bowling alleys. I knew who she was. The most famous girl in Hell. I went up and introduced myself as her grandfather."

"It wouldn't have been fitting to tell her that you had just raped and murdered a young girl, would it have?" Mili shot back.

Morgan shook his head.

"Always with these accusations. Why do you hate me so much, Milicent? I never even so much as *touched* you."

"You didn't need to. Your fascination with Mardie spared me your *attentions*. Nothing else."

"I have to say that Mardie was and still is a beautiful woman. You, on the other hand, were like your mother. Fat and undesirable. I don't know how or when you changed, but somehow you've become real competition for your twin."

"Shut up!" Mili screamed.

"You are such a piece of shite!" Mardie cried and pulled out the long knife she had hidden in her purse.

Morgan was surprised and furious.

"What, Mardie?" he shouted. "Stabbing me once was not enough for you? Shall we replay the scene where the slut daughter murders her seduced father? As good as Shakespeare don't you think?"

"Yes!" Mardie cried. "Show us where I stabbed you."

Morgan ripped open his shirt and revealed his bare chest. A white scar stood out in the middle of his chest. Mili stepped closer. She couldn't see any scar on his neck from Mardie's knife, the real place where she had fatally stabbed Morgan Wickett.

Mili challenged him.

"I don't who you are, but you are not our father. The scar on your chest was given to you by the girl you killed at the kibbutz. There is another scar on your leg."

"That proves nothing," Wickett sneered.

"It proves everything!" Mili cried. "If you were the real Morgan Wickett you would have a scar below the hinge of your jaw where Mardie stabbed and killed him. My guess is that you are the Shapeshifter named Glenn, and now your life is required for rape and murder."

"I am not going to die!" Morgan hollered at Mili. "I am going to live! I have your daughter for protection and I will roam this world without you ever finding us again."

"Demented dreams," Mili shouted back. "You have exactly ten seconds to reveal who you really are."

Wickett scowled deeply.

Mardie began counting loudly down from ten.

"Ten! Nine! Eight! Seven! Six—"

Seemingly at the speed of light Morgan Wickett morphed into a tall Shapeshifter, revealing himself to be the very demon Mili had called out. As he opened his mouth to speak Little Mardie cried "Run!"

Mili understood instantly and pushed Mardie out the open garage door. Pfot shot out as well, looking back as he ran. Lucifer shook his finger at the Shapeshifter who had broken thousands of years of tradition by sexually violating and killing a human. The demon looked at Satan's odd gesture, then smiled. It was a smile of triumph, a smile of having gotten away with it all. Too bad it was premature.

Little Mardie threw her arms up in the air and began to spin. Faster and faster she twirled.

Her father yelled, "Go, girl!" as she burst into a ball of flame.

A star of pure fire glowed where she had stood. The demon's face registered pure terror as he was enveloped in flames. His body exploded into charred fragments of bone and ash and blew out the gallery into the street.

The flames leapt from Little Mardie's body and caught the display cases on fire. They raced along the hose of a welding tank at which point the shop blew to high heaven. Mili, Mardie, and Pfotenhauer ran for cover as burning timbers, chunks of clay and terracotta, even pieces of cement from the shop floor fell with a destructive vengeance. The fire consuming the gallery roared as Lucifer and Little Mardie walked out of the inferno together.

San Francisco fire engines and ambulances arrived sirens screaming, and stayed until the fire was completely doused. After the firemen had wrapped up and driven away, Mili looked at her daughter and simply said, "Explain."

Little Mardie walked over and took her mother's hand.

"First, I am sorry. I spotted that Shapeshifter following me everywhere the last few days. I knew how he looked was somehow significant, but I didn't know that he had put on your father's face. I was not afraid, because I knew I could burn the demon to smithereens the moment he laid a hand on me.

"When he introduced himself at the bowling alley and claimed that he was Morgan Wickett, my grandfather, I was surprised. But I could tell by his walk and talk that the 'man' had never been to England in his life. It had to be that stupid Shapeshifter again. He picked the wrong person to imitate if he wanted to get in my pants."

Mili gasped. Lucifer looked appalled. Little Mardie chuckled.

"Anyway, Mom, I had to see the whole crazy thing through to the end. How he knew about the wormhole in the bowling alley bar, I do not know, but a lot of demons use those by the hundreds, so I shouldn't have been surprised. My bad. I guess the only thing I can say besides I'm sorry again, is that whatever detective bug bit you, it has bitten me, too." Little Mardie's eyes went wide with wonder. "I couldn't stop. I couldn't tell anyone. And I would do it all over again in a heartbeat."

Mili hugged her daughter and everyone clapped. A bit understated perhaps, but most of those gathered were, after all, British. Lucifer put his arms around both his wife and his daughter while Mardie did a bit of a jig and Pfot wiped a few tears away.

A woman came striding toward them down the now empty street, a purposeful quality to her gait. She was dressed in a long, plaid skirt and a brown sweater even in the summer. A San Francisco local, obviously. She walked right up to the small group gathered in front of the ruined garage. She stopped and waved a CD in front of their faces.

"Who are you people?" she asked in a highly displeased New Zealand accent. She was tall and thin, school girl attractive with bobbed brown hair streaked with blonde. She waved the CD again. "This security disc contains images of *you* entering my gallery, starting it on fire, and then running for your lives while it burned to the ground. To the effin' ground!" she shrieked, losing it. "Building gone, workshop gone, gallery gone, and every single antiquity gone." The woman put her hands on her hips and leaned in a bit threateningly. "Who are you?"

Lucifer looked at her and replied calmly.

"My name is Lucifer Morningstar and this is my wife, Milicent, late of Scotland Yard.

This is our daughter, Little Mardie. And her aunt, Mardie Wickett. Last, this is our friend and colleague, Paul Pfotenhauer. We are here because we tracked a criminal to your establishment. In the holocaust that got set off he disappeared. I apologize for the unfortunate situation, and I shall compensate you for every penny of your loss—building, contents, *and* collectibles." Satan smiled winsomely. "Can you estimate the total?"

The gallery owner reached over and offered her hand.

"My name is Caroline Oakes," she declared. "The one-time proprietor of this now incinerated gallery." She gave Lucifer a thin, but real smile. "I appreciate your forthright manner."

"I am sure we can come to some kind of accommodation no matter the expense," Lucifer assured her.

Oakes looked a bit suspicious at his directness. She lived in a city where property issues were incapable of being settled without threading a mind-numbing bureaucratic maze. The only person who'd ever gotten anything done quickly in San Francisco was Dan Brown, and no one cited him as an example to imitate.

"You're serious?" she asked, a bit shrilly. "No fake cash or bounced checks?"

"You have my word," Lucifer said and bowed slightly. "And we can settle right now. Calculate a figure that you believe is fair and we'll go to the closest bank. I'll use a credit card to get proceeds into your hands as fast as the computers can authorize the cash advance."

Caroline studied the Devil's face for a long moment.

"What did you say that your name was?"

"Lucifer."

Caroline squinted her eyes, looked at the Devil, and thought hard.

"Don't know the name," she said finally.

"Didn't you go to Sunday School when you were a little girl?" Satan asked.

"No. Did I miss anything?"

"Not really," Lucifer said and smiled quite pleasantly. "So, then, the nearest bank?"

CHAPTER TWENTY

Pfotenhauer was carefully negotiating the terrible road that led out of New Babylon into the countryside beyond. He knew the exact point when he entered the vast holdings of the Ben-Yehuda Kibbutz. As if by magic the roads were empty of debris and all the holes were filled in and leveled out.

Lucifer sat in the front with Pfot, wearing chinos and a white polo shirt. Pfot had on black slacks, a white dress shirt, and a black-and-white polka-dot bowtie. Mili sat in the back seat with Mardie. Both ladies were dressed in brown shorts and taupe-colored short-sleeved cotton blouses. When Mardie saw Mili's outfit she did a double take, and then remarked, "Check us out," pointing at her sister and then herself. "We could be twins."

Mili didn't react, but Pfotenhauer, who'd overheard Mardie's teasing comment, laughed hysterically, his bony body shaking like a skeleton dangling from some kid's Halloween stick. Up and down, up and down, up and down. Thank God nothing snapped.

"Tell me again why I agreed to come today," Lucifer complained, not pleased at experiencing the longest car ride he'd ever had in Hell.

"Dear husband," Mili answered. "You agreed to come and observe for yourself the influence that a single well-run farming collective has had on Hell's eco-systems."

"And then shut it down."

Mili ignored Lucifer's rude response.

"You are going to meet the people irrigating with clean water, producing healthy fruits and vegetables, and planting so many trees that the air is sweet and pure."

"Not my kind of people."

"Of course they are, love. Kindred souls even."

Lucifer turned in his seat and scowled at Mili.

"Kindred souls only because they're damned."

"Get over yourself, Lu," Mili responded. "Just because God wants it unpleasant down here doesn't mean *you* have to shake your fist at blue skies and step on every wild flower you see."

"I've actually done both of those things."

"Then you should be ashamed of yourself."

Lucifer turned and looked out the front window and sneaked a little smile. He loved pulling Mili's chain once in a while. She was so much smarter than him that the only thing that saved his bacon during their occasional disagreements was to act like Donald Trump and say things that were so outrageous she'd just grimace in frustration.

But of course she was right. He *didn't* have to abide with Hell being so miserable. He secretly liked the idea that it could be improved, and according to Mili he was about to see evidence that such a thing could be done on a large scale. Farmers making the sky blue? Who knew? Satan turned his face back to Mili again.

"Who are the people we're meeting at the collective? Russians?"

"No."

"Turks?"

Mili shook her head.

Lucifer frowned.

"Peruvians?"

170

"No."

"North Koreans?"

"Are you shitting me, Lu?" Mili said and stared daggers at her husband. "I said these farmers made things better, not worse. You want black skies instead of gray, get the North Koreans."

"Sheese lareesh, woman. How many farm collectives can there be?"

"They're everywhere. South America, Central America, Mexico, the Middle East, and almost every nation in Africa."

"So the people running this farm are from one of those places?"

"Yes. They're from Israel."

Lucifer stared at his wife.

"They're Jews? It's a kibbutz?"

"Why are you shouting?" Mili asked.

"You could have just told me without letting me make a fool out of myself."

"I didn't let you. You pretty much signed up on your own."

Satan bit his lip only long enough to keep his temper in check. It would hardly do to incinerate all the people in the car. After a few moments he was ready to carry on.

"Do I know any of the people who run the *kibbutz?*" The Devil pronounced kibbutz slowly and painfully, as if his tongue was suffering from an advanced case of thrush.

"You might, dear," Mili answered with exaggerated politeness. "If you' ever followed politics in Israel."

"Not since the Romans carted off the Temple treasures," Lucifer replied flippantly. "Tried to buy some of that stuff. Vespasian treated me like day old matzo."

"The leaders of the kibbutz are David Ben-Gurion who was the first prime minister of modern Israel, and Moshe Dayan, the greatest general in Israel's modern history."

"And now they're farmers," Satan commented, as though they had sunk to the lowest indignity.

"They were part of the pioneering kibbutz movement in Palestine," Mili continued, "at the beginning of the twentieth century. They performed genuine miracles there, restoring land that had languished for hundreds of years under the control of the Ottoman Turks. Now they are doing the very same thing here in Hell."

"All right. I'm impressed. Or as impressed as I can be with a bunch of Hellions."

Mili flushed and choked with anger, but Mardie jumped in.

"What is this thing you have about disrespecting the damned, Lu? You're hardly in a position to pull a holier-than-thou attitude on the rest of us."

Lucifer's eyebrows shot up and he lashed out at his sister-in-law.

"*You* belong down here, Mardie. We all just spent a couple of horrible days pursuing a particularly pissed off Morgan Wickett, or at least a bloody damn good imitation of him, because your last words to your father were 'Take this!' and you stuck a knife in his neck."

"Well, at least it wasn't God's neck."

Satan felt as though he'd been slapped. But as furious as he was at Mardie's innuendo, he couldn't come up with a good comeback. He decided to sulk until someone apologized to him. He sulked all the way to the kibbutz.

* * *

Despite the tense car ride, Pfot and his passengers put on pleasant faces when they stepped out of the car and were greeted by David Ben-Gurion and Moshe Dayan. Lucifer instantly recognized both men. Ben-Gurion with his fuzzy halo of white hair. And Dayan with his famous eyepatch. There were handshakes and then tea, while the kibbutz leaders talked with Satan about their improvement plans and the results they had achieved so far.

Despite his earlier skepticism, Lucifer was very impressed by the vast truck gardens and the Byzantine system of wells and irrigation installations that had turned Hell's wasteland into forests and farms. The most astonishing transformation, however, was looking up and seeing the sun and a bright blue sky above. It truly overwhelmed him. He had never even imagined that any of this could be possible, yet here it was, accomplished by the unity and hard work of the kibbutzniks.

He was sad to see the blackened remains of the tens of thousands of acres of citrus trees that had been burned to the ground. Mili whispered to him that while he went with Ben-Gurion and Dayan she and Mardie wanted to search for Brigitte's body. It had been discovered, but hastily left behind when the orange groves had first been set on fire.

Lucifer nodded, and Mili and Mardie exited Ben-Gurion's apartment. They left the kibbutz housing and walked into the heaps of burned wood and ash searching for the shallow grave where Brigitte's murdered body had been found. Mili recollected that the spot had not been more than a hundred yards from the kibbutz. And sure enough, Mardie found her bones again. The trees around the grave had burned, and the body itself had had its flesh burned away. But the blackened bones of the victim lay undisturbed.

Mardie walked back to the kibbutz and borrowed a shovel from a workhand. She and Mili took turns digging a deeper grave than the one where the skeleton lay. They moved the bones slowly and carefully, arranging them as though Brigitte needed to approve of their effort. Head bone connected to the neck bones. Neck bones connected to the back bones. Back bones connected to the leg bones. Now hear the word of the Lord. Whatever that meant.

"Should we say anything?" Mili asked.

"Like what?"

"I don't know. I doubt seriously that God hears or cares about anything down here."

"Why would he? This is like the island for misfit toys."

"Ha!" Mili gave her sister a thumbs-up. "Those words are as good as any."

"Really?"

Mili nodded. "But I have a few more to add."

"Would you?" Mardie asked.

Mili nodded, then bowed her head.

"Dear Lord, we are honoring the remains of a girl whose life in Hell was cut short in a terrible way. If you can see it in your heart to let her indeed rest in peace, I and my sister thank you for that charity."

"And while we're at it, God," Mardie picked up, "the Jews on this kibbutz are better people in every way than anyone I ever met on Earth. They are kind and generous, loving to each other, gracious to strangers, and working to turn Hell into Paradise. That stuff counts God, and I think you should rethink their punishment and offer them a transfer to Heaven. Just a suggestion. Amen."

"Amen," echoed Mili. "Nice request. Pretty sure that neither one of our wishes will get much consideration. But, hey, it can't hurt to ask."

Mardie touched her sister's hand, smiled her thanks, then took a turn with the shovel, tossing dirt into Brigitte's grave. Mili wondered if her husband would indeed ask Jehovah for a replacement Hellion body for the damned girl. Some part of her suspected that as Mardie had predicted he was not going to report her disappearance. Her Earthly life had been warped and violent. Her time in Hell lonely and sad. And her second death the stuff of every woman's nightmares.

Hitherto, Lucifer had always reported Hellion losses to God, and brought their replacements back to Hell. But maybe this would be his first exception. She hoped so. Couldn't there finally be a deserved respite for this girl who had suffered so much? She didn't know. Only Lucifer did.

✳ ✳ ✳

Mili was surprised when Lucifer accepted Ben-Gurion's invitation to join the communal dinner at the kibbutz. The dining room looked just like a school cafeteria on Earth, a buffet line with tables and chairs filling up a very large floor. This buffet, however, had choices that were spectacular. Salads with fresh, crunchy vegetables. All kinds of homemade dressings. Hot fresh bread. Roast lamb with garlic and butter. Baked potatoes, boiled peas, steamed broccoli and carrots. And bowls of fresh fruit for dessert, along with coffee and tea.

David Ben-Gurion sat with his wife, Paula, a dark-haired, well-dressed woman. Moshe came in with a gorgeous blonde. When he saw Mardie he went over and gave her a kiss on the cheek and whispered in her ear, "Say the word and I'll dump the bimbo."

The evening's conversation focused on how the kibbutz had been started and expanded over the years. How the pioneers had worked to enrich its soil toiling to raise premium vegetables and fruits. And, of course, how they had planted tens of thousands of fruit trees.

Lucifer listened to every word, all the while commenting on the excellent food. At one point he asked where the lamb had been pastured.

"Bethlehem," Moshe answered. "Some entrepreneurial Christian Arabs have begun importing Scottish Blackface sheep into Israel and you've tasted the quality they've achieved."

"How do you get them down here?"

"We have a contract signed by us and honored by our personal Mammon banker. He arranges to have the sheep brought here, alive and well, for inspection and acceptance."

"So the animals are imported by the demon network?" Lucifer pressed Dayan.

"Can't be sure," Ben-Gurion answered for Moshe. "But how else would they get down here?"

"Have you thought of raising them here?"

175

"Thought of it, indeed, and we hope to when the right time comes. I imagine that will be delayed now while we dedicate ourselves to cleaning the burned groves and planting new trees."

"When did you first observe the blue skies overhead?" Lucifer asked pointing up.

"About three months ago, and we were pretty shocked," Ben-Gurion answered. "Somehow our improvements had been absorbed into the very essence of Hell, *real* terraforming as it were, not just farfetched science fiction."

"It didn't feel very Hell-ish, however," Ben-Gurion added. "While that didn't immediately disturb us, we figured in the long run we'd have some explaining to do to you." The old statesman looked Lucifer in the eyes and waited for his response.

"You're correct," he told Ben-Gurion, wiping his mouth with his napkin and setting it beside his empty plate. "What you have done here challenges the very nature of Hell and threatens to rip the fabric of dark and replace it with light. Never ever in all my years down here have I seen anything like it.

"God imagines that Hell is primarily a state of sorrow," he went on, "because you, and I, and all of us are separated from Him. Understandable theology from his point of view. And if that is the intent of His punishment then we will abide without his presence for all time. Having said that, I don't think there is any reason why Hell can't be cleaned, fixed up, and turned into a pleasant, prosperous place for everyone down here. Until Jehovah decides we've somehow messed up Hell by un-messing it, I have a challenge for your kibbutz, David. What are its holdings in Hell right now?"

Ben-Gurion had not yet had time to absorb Lucifer's positive responses to his kibbutz's success, so he answered slowly, not really understanding where the Master of Hell was leading.

"We have 160,000 acres of gardens and groves."

"And how many folks are required to care for everything and everyone?"

"We could be more efficient with more machines, but right now we have close to ten thousand workers, mostly middle-aged and older folks."

"All right," Lucifer said. "As of this moment—and we'll get it written down and notarized—I am expanding the kibbutz holdings to ten million acres. I will personally provide the equipment that you need. *And* my own administrative organization will help you recruit new kibbutzniks to live here."

Without another word he stood up and extended his hand to Ben-Gurion. David stood and shook it with a look of astonishment on his face. Then Lucifer shook hands with Moshe Dayan who laughed out loud he was so amazed. Lucifer laughed along with him, and in moments everyone in the dining room joined in. Then everyone stood and cheered.

Lucifer nodded modestly, then reached down and picked up his empty plate.

"And now everyone," he said addressing the happy crowd. "If you'll forgive me, I think I'll have some seconds."

✳ ✳ ✳

Lucifer and Mili stayed up late drinking coffee back at David Ben-Gurion's place. He was ecstatic over Lucifer's decision to transform Hell in earnest with his magnanimous gift to the kibbutz. Mrs. Ben-Gurion had gone to bed early and Mili had noticed that Mardie and Moshe were missing in action. Probably an apt description, she thought.

Mili not only noted their absence, but noticed that the fresh air and wonderful food had increased not only her sense of wellbeing, but her libido as well. Odd, but deeply satisfying to re-experience urges that Hell's sheer awfulness often repressed in her. But not here. She found herself watching the time and wondering how long before she could get her spouse into bed.

It didn't happen until long after midnight, but Mili found her dear husband equally amorous and together they pursued their own private socializing until sometime after two. My goodness, Mili thought, quietly afterglowing alongside sleeping Lucifer. She hadn't felt this content since she and Satan had honeymooned on the alternate world where they had pursued Hugh Everett's murderous double. Though they had tried desperately to find the wormhole back to Hell, it had taken seven years and a helping hand from *their* Hugh Everett to do so.

In the meanwhile, they became lovers on their new world, and then spouses, and then parents. Those memories should have clued her into the fact that something special was going on this night between her husband and her womb, but she fell asleep before she got past reminiscing how good the salad had been at dinner, and the broccoli, and the potatoes, and...

CHAPTER TWENTY-ONE

valon Lanes was standing room only for the championship match between The Potentates, Africa's best damned bowling team, and The British Royals, led by former king, former consort, and former playboy, Edward VII. Bertie to his bowling teammates and girlfriends. The pretentious fat man with fingers as thick as the klobasse sausages from his mother's home town of Hanover, Germany, had earlier in the week bowled Hell's first ever three-hundred-pin Perfect Game to beat The American Presidents and lead his team into the final.

Lucifer had decided to let a Samn demon take his place as contest judge and sat in the gallery with his lovely wife, Milicent, and his spoiled child, Little Mardie. All three of them were eating ice cream from the first-of-its-kind Ben and Jerry's booth at the bowling alley. In fact, everyone in the bowling alley was eating ice cream.

Sitting next to Mili was her sister Mardie. Next to her was President Theodore Roosevelt. He was eating chocolate and marshmallow ice cream and humming "Happy Days Are Here Again." This caused considerable annoyance to his daughter Alice, seated alongside of him eating strawberry cheesecake ice cream. She associated that mindless tune with TR's cousin, Franklin, whom she called the endless president. Goddamn Democrat.

Lucifer was enjoying the excitement of the crowd. My God. Bowling *and* ice cream. He looked tenderly at Mili. She saw him and smiled back.

"I have to confess, love," he told her, "that your decision to open ice cream shops in Hell was progressive genius."

"Really?"

Lucifer reached over and squeezed Mili's hand.

"Yes. You are not only beautiful and brilliant, you also have a big heart."

"I also have a big debt thanks to the one hundred percent interest rate your bank is charging me."

Lucifer arched an eyebrow.

"I didn't know you were the actual borrower," he explained. "You hid your ownership in a veritable landfill of dummy companies." He gazed into Mili's eyes for a moment. "Who helped you do that?"

"Shouldn't say."

"Never know when you might have to fool your husband again?"

"Maybe," Mili replied coyly.

Lucifer wrinkled his forehead and thought about that for a second. "Interest remains at one hundred percent."

"Ha!" Mili laughed. "Enjoy your ice cream."

Little Mardie had gone wandering only to return to her seat in a foul mood. Her aunt looked at her and tried to cheer her up.

"What's the matter, doll?" Mardie asked.

Her niece's cranky face softened to a sad and wistful one.

"The hole in space that used to be in the corner by the bar is not there anymore."

"Maybe your father deemed it unsafe to leave it open. That Shapeshifter who pretended he was your grandfather may not have been the only creature down here with ill intentions regarding you."

Little Mardie shrugged.

"I can protect myself."

"Well, of course you can," Mardie agreed. "But as brave and confident as you are, demons and every inhabitant of Hell now know that you are vulnerable, and that under certain circumstances you could be hurt, even killed."

Little Mardie looked at her aunt.

"Are you giving me advice?"

"No. Just reminding you, that like all of us down here, you are eternal, but mortal, just like your mother and your father. Hell is undergoing a lot of changes, and exercising a little caution during the process is probably prudent."

"You talk kinda like a school teacher."

"I'll take that as a compliment, thank you." Mardie straightened up in her chair. "I haven't always talked this way."

Little Mardie stared at her aunt.

"Do you have any stories you want to share?" she asked.

"When you're eighteen," Mardie answered.

"I have to wait five years?"

"Yes, but you can eat ice cream the whole time you're waiting. Best thing for a girl your age."

Mardie leaned over and hugged her namesake.

"Later on, it's booze, smokes, and boys," she said.

"Really?"

"Yes, indeed. But you'll still like ice cream, too."

Mili was watching the two bowling teams assemble at their lanes. The Potentates looked particularly confident. Especially blind Idi Amin who had managed to roll *two* Perfect Games in the semifinal match against The European Dictators. *That* would not be happening again. Lucifer had carefully questioned the two little Pixie's who performed maintenance on the pin reset machines in the bowling alley. Thoughtful questioning had included Satan's threat to rip off a leg from one, and actually grabbing the arms of the other and beginning to pull waiting for the confession that came in the nick of time.

The second Pixie confessed that she had rigged the software controlling the reset to place several pins in slightly more advantageous positions for achieving strikes, but only when Idi Amin bowled. Satan ordered the now repentant Pixie to reboot the reset programs to give The British Royals team the advantage Amin had enjoyed. For which members of the team, the Pixie asked? All of them, Satan commanded. Take that Idi Amin.

Mili looked at her sister sitting next to her. Mardie looked a bit down, a pensive expression on her face.

"What's the matter, hon?" Mili asked. "Bowling just not your thing?"

"No, it's not that," Mardie answered. "I have to admit that encountering the Shapeshifter wearing our father's image seems to have stirred up the past for me. I never thought anything could hurt me down here, but Brigitte's rape and murder has ruined my life. How many Morgan Wicketts are there down here, human *or* demon, just waiting for their chance? Every day, I worry. Every night, I have nightmares. There's no escape."

Mili took Mardie's hand in hers.

"I promise I will track Morgan down and bring him to Lucifer for justice."

"I just want him gone."

"Do you remember the hole by the bar that took us straightaway to San Francisco?"

"Little Mardie told me that Lucifer had sealed it up."

"No. Those things can't be sealed up. Best one can do is move the opening through some kind of manipulation of gravity. The hole has been moved *behind* the bar."

"And?"

"And its maw has a date with our father."

"I could let that cheer me up," Mardie said tentatively.

"Yes, you could. And there's no need to talk to Lucifer about our project to dispose of Morgan. Just a little improvement to Hell of our own."

"But won't he still be a threat to women on Earth?"

"Not if we have him tossed down the chute as a different entity than the one he is now."

"You mean cut his penis off?"

"Significantly modified at any rate," Mili answered speaking quietly. "And we'll have the plastic surgeon add breasts and hips and arrange a new identity that will allow her to live life in such a way that she will truly understand what it's like to be a female."

"Oh, my."

"Oh, yes."

"The Wickett sisters in Hell give their father a makeover."

Both Mili and Mardie laughed hysterically.

"Oh, dear God," Mardie uttered. "I can't believe how lucky I was to be sent to Hell."

"You and me both, babe," Mili said, happily. "You and me both."

✳ ✳ ✳

Mili lay in the darkness next to Lucifer. They were on their backs holding hands. Lu was very quiet, making an effort to internalize the fact that The British Royals had claimed the tournament crown by throwing a Perfect Series, that is, three sets with all four bowlers throwing two Perfect Games. There was no such thing as a Perfect Series. Lucifer had to make up the term. Not that he wasn't pleased that Idi Amin and The Potentates had been humiliatingly defeated by all those Perfect Games. But it felt a little like too much of a good thing. Like having sex with Mili twelve times in a row. No, no, that wasn't a good comparison. He would never turn down that experience. He squeezed Mili's hand.

"How are you faring, dear one?" she asked tenderly.

"I was thinking how great our lovemaking was the night we stayed over at the kibbutz." Lucifer rolled on his side and stroked Mili's cheek. "I think I would have enjoyed a few encores."

Mili rolled over into her husband's welcoming arms.

"No need, sweet love," she whispered. "Once was all it took."

Lucifer held his wife and tried to figure out what she meant. She'd always been ready for a second ride on the merry-go-round, why not then? Unless…

"Are you pregnant, Mili?"

"Yes. I'll need to have a check-up sooner or later, but I know that we have a little boy on the way."

"A boy!" Lucifer repeated ecstatic.

"Yes, and since you let me name Little Mardie after my sister, you get to pick the name for our son."

"Oh, man, how great is that?" Satan exclaimed. "How about something Biblical, like Saul, or Jeremiah, or Nebuchadnezzar?"

Mili giggled loudly at the last choice.

"What about picking a name that signals our great hope for the future of Hell and its new reality?" she asked.

"A righteous thought, my brilliant wife," the Devil replied. "You know I don't use that word indiscriminately. We are going to have blue skies down here, clean water, healthy food, and fine metropolises complete with Ben and Jerry's ice cream shops. Might even have a chance at getting Al Gore down here now."

Mili lay quietly in her husband's tender embrace waiting for Lucifer to share the name her son would receive. She didn't have to wait long.

"I've got it, love," Lucifer announced. "The first boy born in Hell will be named Sriracha."

"What?" Mili asked in disbelief.

"Sriracha! It's a hot sauce."

Mili cried. Lucifer laughed. And Sriracha gave his mom a good kick in the ribs. No, she thought. That's impossible. Sriracha assured his mother that it was truly him by giving her another kick. Ow, Mili thought, and then realized—as if she were experiencing a prophetic vision—that if Hell cleaned up the way David Ben-Gurion and Moshe Dayan promised it could, then lots of other people might find themselves expectant parents. Gracioous God.

Mili nibbled on Lucifer's ear and whispered, "Expect a Balaam banker to visit you in the next few days, seeking your approval for a loan to start up another chain of businesses down here. This one with a community service orientation."

"*Nothing* says community service like ice cream," he said.

"Well, actually, one tops it, I think," Mili disagreed. "And it's going to be a very popular destination."

"I'm waiting."

"I'm working on a name for it," Mili explained.

"Oh, ho! So it's another Milicent Wickett enterprise?"

"Yes. I think I'll call it Candy's Condoms. I love the galaxy of double entendres that name generates."

"I'm sure you're right," Lucifer happily agreed. "What's a condom?"

The End

ACKNOWLEDGEMENTS

I would like to thank the faithful friends of Mili and Mardie Wickett who have faithfully followed them through Hell!

Particularly Bobette Jones, who read and encouraged me on the earliest drafts of this book and its predecessor; perfectionist copy editor Jerry Sexton; eagle-eye Mark Meyer of Professional Book Proofreading; Vincent Chong for his unmatchable cover design and art; and lastly, my continuing appreciation to my publisher and friend Lionel A. Blanchard for hanging in there.

CPSIA information can be obtained
at www.ICGtesting.com
Printed in the USA
BVHW05*2230080718
521093BV00009B/153/P